PUFFIN BOOKS

AURORA AND THE LITTLE BLUE CAR

You may already know all about Aurora, because she was in another Young Puffin called *Hallo Aurora!* In which case you will know that things were a bit different in her family – her mother went to an office every day and her nice father stayed at home to write, and to look after Aurora and her little brother, Socrates.

Sometimes though, it seemed almost as if Aurora was the one who looked after Father, because he was inclined to daydream and she had to be practical. For instance, when he let all the woollies blow off the balcony *she* was the one who collected them, when he went into town on the tram *she* reminded him to take the fare from the jam-jar in the kitchen, and perhaps the most important thing of all, she was the only person who kept calm when Father had just passed his driving test and was nervous of driving alone in their little blue car with the red mudguards.

Yes, Aurora was a great help, and she was a very contented little girl too, because she was kept so busy and interested helping with baby Socrates, and joining in all the fun of this happy Norwegian Family.

Anne-Cath. Vestly has a lively, easy way of writing, and her affection for Aurora's loving and united family shines through all the stories in the most appealing way, making all her readers love them too.

For readers of seven to nine, or to be read aloud to listeners of five and six.

Anne-Cath. Vestly was born in 1920 and is married with two sons. Her ambition was to be an actress and she was a member of a theatre group for five years. During this time she started a series of weekly radio programmes for young children. She has now written numero⸻ ⸻ ⸻ ⸻ been translated into many ⸻

Another book by Anne-Cath. Vestly
HALLO AURORA!

ANNE-CATH. VESTLY

Aurora and the Little Blue Car

Translated from the Norwegian by Eileen Amos
Illustrated by Gunvor Edwards

PUFFIN BOOKS

Puffin Books, Penguin Books Ltd, Harmondsworth, Middlesex, England
Viking Penguin Inc., 40 West 23rd Street, New York, New York 10010, U.S A
Penguin Books Australia Ltd, Ringwood, Victoria, Australia
Penguin Books Canada Limited, 2801 John Street, Markham, Ontario, Canada L3R 1B4
Penguin Books (N.Z.) Ltd, 182–190 Wairau Road, Auckland 10, New Zealand

—

First published in Norway under the title *Aurora og den Vesle Bla Bilen*
by Tiden Norsk Forlag 1968
This translation first published by Longman Young Books 1974
Published in Puffin Books 1978
Reprinted 1986

—

Copyright © Tiden Norsk Forlag, 1968
This translation copyright © Longman Young Books, 1974
Illustrations copyright © Longman Young Books, 1974
All rights reserved

—

Made and printed in Great Britain by
Hazell Watson & Viney Limited,
Member of the BPCC Group,
Aylesbury, Bucks
Set in Monotype Ehrhardt

Contents

1. Danger – Falling Stones!

THERE were many blocks of flats at Tiriltoppen, and perhaps some people thought they all looked exactly the same, but that was only because they didn't know them. As a matter of fact all the blocks were different. Block Z, for example, was quite unlike all the others, both inside and out. Outside, it was a rather darker grey than the others and in rainy weather it became even darker, which made it look much nicer; and inside, it had a little girl called Aurora, and that was something the other blocks hadn't got.

Aurora had a little brother called Socrates. Socrates had grown big enough to sit up in his pram, and Aurora was often allowed to mind him out of doors and then they could talk to each other. She could talk to Socrates about almost everything.

Aurora's father was very good at running the house, and he found time as well to study the history of the Ancient Greeks. Just now, however, something else was occupying his mind, and that was learning to drive.

He had had a good many lessons already, and every other afternoon he went down into the town to learn more. The children's mother was home from the office then, so it was quite all right for him to go.

Aurora often waited for Father to come home for it was so exciting to hear how he had got on. He didn't tell anyone but Aurora.

In the evening, while Mother was feeding Socrates, Father came into Aurora's room and described everything he had done in the last lesson, and it wouldn't have taken long for her to know as much about driving as he did.

'I drove in very heavy traffic today,' said Father, 'and I almost managed on my own.'

'Didn't your instructor say anything?' asked Aurora. 'Yes, one or two things,' said Father, 'but I don't think he need have done for I really knew them. Now I must concentrate on learning the highway code, for I think it won't be long before I take the driving test and then, you see, I must know everything that's in this book. It's a great pity you can't read, Aurora, for you could have heard me.'

'Mm,' said Aurora, 'but if you tell me something today I'll remember it tomorrow, and then I can hear you because it's not certain that you'll remember yourself.'

'No,' said Father, 'what you mean is that it's quite certain that I won't.'

And so Father sat and read aloud to Aurora every single evening. Mother thought he was reading fairy stories, but if she had peeped round the door she would have heard something quite different. 'Before moving off, the driver must make sure that the vehicle complies with the regulations. He must see that the brakes are in good order and that he has a clear view in front and behind.'

Sometimes Father used difficult words like condenser, dynamo, battery and so on, and then

Aurora had to say these strange words to herself many times a day so as not to forget them. She had no idea what they meant, but she could repeat them to Father and he had to say what he thought they were. Father probably didn't know so very much about them either, but he could reel them off all the same.

One day Uncle Brande came to see them. He had helped to look after them in the winter when

Father was ill, and Father had said he was a bit wild but very nice all the same. Now he was going to leave town and live in a little hut and do nothing but write. Today he had come to say good-bye.

Mother went into the kitchen and cut up a whole loaf of bread. 'Edward,' she said, 'perhaps you'll bath Socrates this evening because I'd like to make a really nice supper.' While she was in the kitchen and Father was bathing Socrates, Uncle Brande had a talk with Aurora on her own.

'How do you think Daddy is getting on with his driving?' he asked.

'Quite well,' said Aurora, 'but he doesn't know the road signs properly.'

'Just as I thought,' said Uncle Brande, 'and so I made these before I left home.'

He went out and fetched his bag, and it was crammed full of small sheets of cardboard. He had painted all the traffic signs, and made a hole in them and put a string through so they could be hung up.

Now he and Aurora got busy. They made haste to hang up STOP over the front door, and GIVE WAY AT MAJOR ROAD on the inside of Aurora's door, and DANGER – FALLING STONES under the shelf in the hall because it was so full of caps and scarves and gloves. Father hadn't had time to deal with all these woollen things yet.

They put SLIPPERY ROAD and SHEET ICE on the kitchen floor, and ROAD WORKS in the living-room, because Father was so terribly busy that he wasn't as good at tidying up as he used to be.

NO THROUGH ROAD was on the balcony door, and that was a good idea in case anyone should think they could go out and get down on to the hill that way from the tenth floor. Both DANGEROUS BEND and CROSSROADS pointed from the living-room into the hall, because the way to the kitchen and the way to the bathroom and the way to Aurora's room and the way to the living-room all met there. In front of Socrates' play-pen they put LEVEL CROSSING WITH GATES, and where Socrates usually crawled when he wasn't in his play-pen they put LEVEL CROSSING WITHOUT GATES.

There were a great many notices, for Uncle Brande really had made every sign there was, and when Father came out of the bathroom with Socrates, he stopped short. Socrates didn't understand this at all. At this point Father ought to have gone into the kitchen and said, 'Socrates must have something to eat now.'

Both Mother and Father usually spoke gently to him because they were a bit afraid that he might get angry with them if he didn't have his food quickly enough. But today Father just walked about muttering, and then stood still and spoke out loud, and as far as Socrates could discover there wasn't a single word about food. It was just something like 'No entry' and a lot of other words that Socrates didn't understand, but in any case he knew that they weren't going to satisfy his hunger.

And so he set up his loudest wail, and Father gave a start and repeated, 'Give way to military vehicles, fire-engines, ambulances, police cars and troops on the march.'

Mother took Socrates from him and said, 'Edward, will you get the sandwich dish? Uncle Brande can take the cups and the tea, Aurora can carry the plates, and I'll bring the porridge and Socrates.'

Socrates thought this almost sounded like food, so he stopped howling, and when Mother sat down with him at the end of the table, he bent over the porridge plate and Mother filled him up as fast as she could.

The others began to eat as well, and Aurora

realized that Uncle Brande had come partly because he was hungry too. The dish was piled with sandwiches – and suddenly they had all gone.

Uncle Brande's face was happy and contented behind his beard. He said he was looking forward to taking up his writing seriously once more, because in the town there was so much to hinder him. He loved being in the country; potatoes were cheap there, so food would be no problem, and if he was short of money he could do a bit of work on one of the neighbouring farms.

All the same, Mother didn't seem quite sure that Uncle Brande would manage, because she gave him several tins of sardines and one of rissoles to take away with him, although she hadn't very much of that kind of thing herself.

Father gave him a packet of tobacco which pleased him even better, for when he had put it in his pocket he looked as if he had nothing more to wish for and hadn't a care in the world.

Before Uncle Brande left, he and Father whispered together. 'Don't you be too sure,' laughed Father, 'before you know where you are, I shall be driving out to see you.'

'By the way,' said Uncle Brande, 'if you people are at a loss for a baby-sitter one day, just let me know.'

'Thanks very much,' said Father.

The next day Father realized that one of the signs had certainly been put in the right place, for just when Socrates was having his morning nap, and Aurora was outside playing in the sandpit, and Mother was at the office as usual, and he himself was going to sit down and read – gloves and scarves and caps came tumbling down on his head as he went by the shelf in the hall, exactly where it said 'Danger – falling stones'.

Father stood and looked at the heap on the floor. He thought he remembered seeing the housewives in the block hanging their woollens out to air in the yard some weeks ago.

There was a terribly high wind today, thought Father. He had better put them out on the balcony. If they lay there in the hot sun, any moths that had thought of making the gloves their summer home would disappear.

No sooner said than done. Father carried outside all the woollens they possessed, and there were plenty of them. He went to the wardrobe and fetched their sweaters and jackets and hung them over the edge of the balcony, and when there was no more room there he had to take out two stools and spread clothes on them too. The things would be all right there and he could leave them for an hour or two while he studied the highway code. The sooner he took that driving test, the sooner he could begin to read history again. Soon afterwards he was sitting with the book in front of him reading aloud, for in that way he remembered it more easily.

'A driver must have his horse under control and make sure that it is securely tied up if he leaves his vehicle. In winter the horse must have bells on its harness.'

There really were a great many things one had to know if one wanted to learn to drive a car. Father gave a little sigh, but then he began to think about that horse that had to have bells on its harness, and suddenly he remembered how, long ago when he was a small boy, he had sat between his mother and father wrapped in a big fur rug and ridden in a horse-drawn sleigh. It was a sparkling cold night and there were stars in the sky. The horse had trotted away so gaily, the rocking of the sleigh had been so soothing, and at last his eyes had closed and he had fallen asleep, and although he was asleep he had seemed to see the stars the whole time. Father leant back in his chair, heard the sleigh-bells ring, and closed his eyes.

Father slept and Socrates slept and out on the balcony there was bright sunshine. Then the wind came. First of all it played with a glove, and then with another one, and with a scarf, and perhaps it thought that it would help the sun to drive away the moths and maggots. But the trouble with the wind was that it soon became too boisterous. At first it thought it was fun just to keep the gloves and sweaters and scarves moving, but then it wanted to lift them up into the air. It blew so hard that at length something sailed out from the balcony on the tenth floor. It was a thick glove, so the wind blew harder still, and the glove flew in to the balcony of a flat two floors below, right on to the head of a lady who had just set up her easel because she was thinking of painting a picture that day.

She gave a little start as the glove came tumbling down, but when she felt her head and found that a small red and white glove had landed on it, she realized that it was nothing to worry about. She looked up to see where it had come from and gasped quite loudly, for there, two floors above her, scarves and sweaters were flapping about, and the arms of the sweaters waved to her, and the scarves twisted and turned as if they were saying 'Now we're going to jump – shall we? shan't we? Yes, off we go!' And they floated out into the air, more gracefully than the glove had done, and sailed away. The wind caught them again and whirled them round. A thin white sweater fell into a big sand-pit. The sand was damp and the sweater didn't stay white for long. It was covered with brown blotches and looked more like a giraffe.

In that sand-pit, Aurora was sitting playing with her little car. She had brought three cars with her today because she knew that if her friends Brit-Karen and Nusse came along, they

would be sure to want to play with them, and then she would be allowed to have a turn at pushing Nusse's beautiful dolls' pram.

At the moment the pram was standing still because the doll was asleep, and Aurora was showing Nusse and Brit-Karen how to approach a crossroads.

Then the sweater came floating down. All three of them stared at it and Nusse said, 'It's from your place, Aurora, and it's not allowed. You're not allowed to air clothes on the balcony.'

Aurora looked up at all the things that were fluttering and flying, and at those that were still hanging there and hadn't begun to fly yet.

'We must tell Daddy,' she said. The other two followed her, but Aurora was not the first to reach her father.

Father was sitting dreaming about sleigh-bells ringing, when suddenly quite a different bell rang, the front door bell. Socrates had been hearing it for some time and was lying there talking about it.

'That's not sleigh-bells,' said Father and woke up.

He wasn't a little boy any longer. He was a grown-up father who had a son and a daughter, and the worst of it was that he had slept away the time when he ought to have been reading and learning. He went to open the door. There stood a lady who waved a glove in his face.

It was some time before Father understood what was happening. At first he wondered if this was something new that had begun in the flats – waving in people's faces. The lady looked kind and friendly. Father waved back, for he wasn't quite awake yet and he was always very polite.

'This fell on my head,' the lady said, 'but it didn't hurt, it's so soft.'

'Yes,' said Father. 'I was sitting reading.'

'I thought so,' she said. 'You obviously haven't noticed that most of your things are flying about outside.'

'Oh, dear,' said Father. 'That glove is mine. I mean, it belongs to Socrates.'

There was a patter of feet along the corridor. 'Daddy, Daddy, it's not allowed,' said Aurora. 'Nusse and Brit-Karen say that a lot of people will be complaining about you, and just look at Mummy's white sweater!'

Father looked at the white sweater.

'*I* shan't complain,' said the lady. 'I just thought it was amusing,' and she went away again. Father went out on to the balcony to have a look.

'There are still a few things here,' he said, and picked up a thick jacket that belonged to him. It was so heavy that the wind had had to give up, but when he looked down at the hill far below he seemed to see red and blue and white and green garments everywhere.

'We'll fetch them, Daddy,' said Aurora.

'Thank you very much,' said Father, 'that's very kind of you.'

He sighed and went back to his highway code, but two floors beneath him a lady stood on her balcony painting a picture. She looked very pleased as she peered over the edge and painted away, for far down below on the hill three little girls were running about, and when she saw them from above like this it looked almost as if they were picking flowers. The lady just hoped they would find plenty so that it would be some time before they came up again.

When they came back with all the clothes, Father put them back on the shelf, and that same evening Mother found time to wrap them up in bags and newspapers and put them away in a chest.

So there was no more danger from falling stones in Aurora's home but they still didn't take down the sign. It would have to hang there until Father came home one day and said that he had passed his driving test.

2. Secret Signs

FATHER took the highway code with him everywhere. One day when he was giving Socrates his feed, he had put it down on top of the kitchen cupboard. It was clear that Socrates was beginning to get tired of that book because he thought it took some of Father's attention away from him. So he grabbed the spoon and a big blob of porridge fell on the page just where it said what lights a car had to have. Socrates smiled contentedly when he had done this.

That day, Mother said to Aurora, 'I think Daddy is going to take his test soon. It may even be tomorrow, but I don't think he'll tell us. Has he said anything to you?'

'No,' said Aurora, 'only that it will be soon.'

'He stayed up late reading the highway code last night,' said Mother. 'He tried to hide it inside his Greek history book but I saw it all the same.'

'Did you say anything?' asked Aurora.

'No,' answered Mother. 'I think he wants it to be a secret.'

'Yes,' said Aurora, 'because if he doesn't pass he won't need to say anything about it.'

'No,' said Mother, 'but I've told him that I

didn't pass the first time either, and I only just managed it the second time.'

'We won't say anything,' said Aurora.

'We'll pretend not to notice,' said Mother. 'The only thing I'm wondering about is what he means to do with you and Socrates if he has to go and take the test in the morning.'

'He's sure to think of something,' said Aurora, but she was a little anxious, for perhaps Daddy was so taken up with his driving that he had forgotten her and Socrates.

Evening came. Father came home from his driving lesson just as he had done on the other evenings. He didn't say anything, only sat there looking a little dejected.

'You must have something to eat now, Edward,' said Mother.

'No thank you,' said Father, 'I'm not so very hungry.'

A little later on he said, 'It's possible that Uncle Brande may come and see us tomorrow.'

'Hasn't he gone away, then?' asked Mother surprised.

'Oh yes, but he has to come into town to-morrow so I said it would be nice if he could come here because I'm going out myself. I have to go to the University among other things, and fetch something.'

'Oh yes,' said Mother, 'it will be a good idea for him to come, then.'

She said no more, but she couldn't help smiling and so she jumped up from the table and went into the kitchen.

'I'll do the washing-up today, Edward,' she said. 'You get on with your reading.'

'Thanks very much,' said Father, 'that's kind of you.'

Aurora went to bed, and Father came in as usual.

'Daddy,' said Aurora, 'do you remember that bit about the horse?'

'The horse?' said Father.

'Yes, you read it aloud to me yesterday evening,' said Aurora.

'Oh yes,' said Father. 'A horse must be tied up securely if it is left, and in winter it must have bells on its harness.'

'That's good, Daddy,' said Aurora. 'You needn't tell me anything today, I'm so tired.'

'Thank you,' said Father, and went away.

Aurora lay there and thought about the horse. It would be fun to do the same thing with cars, too: fasten them with a rope, and put bells on them in winter, tiny little bells that would jingle as they went along. Suppose all the cars had them . . .

Then Mother came in too.

'We won't say anything, Aurora,' she said, 'but I think it's quite certain.'

'Yes,' said Aurora. 'Shall we make a cake for Daddy tomorrow?'

'All right,' said Mother. 'Uncle Brande can do it if he likes, but supposing Daddy doesn't pass?'

'Then he'll need cake more than ever,' said Aurora.

'That's right, Aurora,' said mother. 'Goodnight.'

The next morning Father still didn't say anything about what he was going to do, but it was a good thing the others knew because he needed help with one or two things.

He managed to see to Socrates and the children's washing as usual, but he couldn't rightly remember what he was to wear himself. Mother brought him a shirt and tie.

'Why do I have to be so smart?' said Father suspiciously.

'Well, I just thought you were going into town,' said Mother, 'so I took the other one you were wearing and put it to be washed.'

'Yes of course,' said Father, 'if you say so.'

'Wouldn't you like a lift into town with me?' asked Mother.

'No,' said Father. 'I don't need to start so early, and I'll wait until Uncle Brande comes so that I know Aurora and Socrates have someone with them.'

'Fine,' said Mother. 'Good-bye, have a nice day.'

'The same to you,' said Father. He looked absolutely miserable. It almost hurt Aurora to look at him.

She hardly dared speak to him as he sat there reading. When Socrates began to yell in the bedroom, Aurora went in to him and sang him to sleep.

Shortly afterwards, Uncle Brande arrived and said, 'I hope I'm not late, Edward.'

'Not at all,' said Father. 'I shall be in good time.'

'Have you got money for the tram?' asked Aurora.

'The tram?' said Father absent-mindedly.

'There's some money in the jam-jar in the kitchen,' said Aurora.

'Oh yes,' said Father.

Uncle Brande slapped him on the back; 'Good luck!' he said.

'So long!' said Father and went to the door.

'I'll go down in the lift with you,' said Aurora.

In the lift she held Father's hand the whole time. She squeezed it as hard as she could, but didn't say anything.

'Have a good time, Aurora,' said Father. He

sounded as if he were going on a long, long journey and many years would pass before he saw her again.

'You'll be coming home to dinner, won't you?' said Aurora.

'Oh yes,' said Father. 'I shall come home in any case, you can rely on that.'

He went out of the block and Aurora ran up again to Uncle Brande.

'You'd better put on Daddy's apron,' she said to him, 'because you're going to make a cake.'

'Am I ?' asked Uncle Brande.

'Yes, because if things go right it will be so nice for Daddy, and if they don't we can eat it just the same.'

'I didn't think you and Mummy knew anything about this,' said Uncle Brande. 'Edward said he hadn't told you.'

'He hasn't,' said Aurora, 'we're just guessing.'

'Well, well,' said Uncle Brande, 'I haven't said anything. Shall we look at the cookery book ?'

He and Aurora found a beautiful cake to make.

'We need eggs and cream,' said Uncle Brande, 'we shall have to go shopping, and I had thought of sweeping the floors.'

'I can go to the supermarket quite well by myself,' said Aurora.

'Fine,' said Uncle Brande. Aurora took a little basket and went off.

She was anxious to know whether a little girl called Tiny who was sometimes outside the store with Puff, her black poodle, would be there again today. It was a long while since she had seen them.

When she got to the supermarket, the dog was there, and Aurora went over to him and said, 'Hallo, Puff!' Just then a big boy came out of the shop and went up to the dog. 'Come on, Puff,

we're going now,' he said. There was no little
girl with him. Perhaps he was Tiny's big
brother, thought Aurora.

But inside the shop she did meet someone she

knew, and that was the old country-woman who
had helped her and Father when they first went
shopping there. They had become good friends
now, and Aurora was allowed to call her Gran,
although of course she wasn't really her Granny.

Gran was having driving lessons too, at the same driving-school as Father.

'Gran,' said Aurora, 'do you know something?'

'Yes, I think I do,' said Gran, 'because I was having a driving lesson yesterday and it looked to me as if what I'm thinking about was going to happen soon.'

'Yes,' said Aurora, 'Daddy hasn't told us, you know, but I think it's certain.'

'If all goes well with him, I thought of making some waffles,' said Gran, 'but it would be a bit out of place to arrive with them if he's been unlucky.'

'Mm,' said Aurora.

'I can send our Morten along with a parcel,' said Gran.

'Who is Morten?' asked Aurora.

'One of my grandsons,' said Gran. 'He knows where you live because he has a friend in the same block.'

'Has he?' said Aurora.

'Can't you put something outside the door if he has passed?' said Gran. 'And if he hasn't passed, there won't be anything there.'

'What shall I put?' asked Aurora. 'A chair?'

'No, it's got to be something your family won't notice,' said Gran.

'I can put a little stick there,' said Aurora.

'That's a good idea,' said Gran. 'I'll keep my fingers crossed for him all day.'

'So will I,' said Aurora. 'Do you think it will help?'

'Of course it will,' said Gran.

Aurora went home with the eggs and cream, and she and Uncle Brande began to beat them. They beat for five minutes each, and their arms ached a bit, but they got on splendidly. Uncle Brande had greased a tin, and the cake went into the oven.

Now there wasn't much else to do but wait. They didn't want to go out, for just think what it would be like if Father came home and there was no one there.

Uncle Brande sat down to read, and Aurora thought she would like to give Daddy something that she had made herself. She would draw a picture. She drew a big car, and behind the steering-wheel in the car a man sat driving it. That was Daddy, and beside him was a lady, and that was Mummy. In the back sat Uncle Brande with a beard, and Socrates and herself.

She hid the drawing in the cupboard, for if Daddy hadn't passed the test she wouldn't give it to him. When she was in the cupboard she crossed her fingers hard and thought and thought about Daddy.

The hours went by and there was no sign of

Father, but as dinner time approached they saw Mother coming. She got out of the car and ran up to the block. 'Has he come home?' she said as soon as she got inside.

Aurora shook her head. Uncle Brande shook his head too. 'Mm, it smells good in here,' said Mother.

'Cake,' said Aurora. 'We've put cream in it, and slices of banana and nuts on top on one side because I said I didn't like them much in cakes, and so Uncle Brande said that he wouldn't put them all over it.'

'That's spendid,' said Mother. 'Perhaps we'd better wait a bit before we have our meal.'

'Here he comes!' shouted Aurora. They all looked out of the window.

There was Father. He looked up at the sky as he walked along, and from time to time he stopped.

'Oh dear!' said Mother. 'He isn't walking very straight. Don't ask any questions, just behave as if nothing had happened.'

'Of course,' said Uncle Brande, 'you'll just see how good I am at behaving naturally.'

As Father came in, Uncle Brande was there immediately. 'So glad you're home, Edward! You know what it's like when you've got dinner ready and the guests don't come. Of course I'm not as good a cook as you are, but I hope it will be all right.'

Father tried to say something, but Uncle Brande was so taken up with behaving naturally that he talked twice as much as usual.

Aurora didn't get the chance to say anything either, but she went up to Father and took his hand, and Mother smiled at him, and Socrates, who was in her arms, reached out to him.

'Come to Daddy,' said Father. 'Do you know something, Socrates? Bsbsbsbsbsbsbsbs. No, of course you don't. Now, how shall I begin? It's spring outside and almost summer, Marie. Just think, I hadn't noticed that until today.'

'No, you've had so much to do,' said Mother. 'Let's eat now.'

'Mm,' said Father. 'There's something you don't know. I don't know whether to tell you or not. I – I passed my driving test today.'

'What?' said Mother, for now she really was surprised. She had been so sure that he hadn't managed it when he began to talk about spring and summer.

'Daddy, have you really passed?' said Aurora. 'Are you quite sure?'

'Of course,' said Father.

'Congratulations!' said Uncle Brande. 'What a good thing we made a cake!'

Aurora darted out of the room and into her

bedroom and fetched a little stick which she put outside the front door. Then she went into her bedroom again and fetched her drawing.

'Congratulations, Daddy!' she said.

'It was a funny thing,' said Father, 'but I drove off and oddly enough I wasn't nervous and I could think clearly. Would you believe it, I was asked about those very lights that Socrates had spilled the porridge on in the book. But I got on all right. It was just as though someone was wishing me luck today.'

'I was keeping my fingers crossed,' said Aurora.

'Did you know I was going to take the test today?' asked Father. 'Did Uncle Brande tell tales?'

'No,' said Aurora, 'but we guessed all the same.'

'Did you go to the University?' asked Uncle Brande.

'No, I forgot all about it,' said Father. 'I can

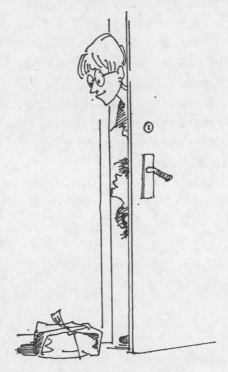

go later. Perhaps I'll take the car and run down there. I can take you to the bus at the same time.'

'Thanks very much, but don't put yourself out for me,' said Uncle Brande.

'It's no trouble,' said Father.

There was a ring at the door. Outside was a round brown paper parcel, but there was no one to be seen.

'To a man who can drive from a friend from the wood,' was written on the parcel.

Father smiled broadly.

'I think I know who it is,' he said. 'You must come with me and see her one of these days, Marie. But how in the world did she know that I passed my test today?'

Aurora didn't say anything, but soon afterwards she went outside and fetched the stick, for Father had better not see secret signs of this kind outside their door.

3. For the First Time

WHEN they had drunk their coffee and eaten a
lot of cake and waffles, it was time for Father to
drive into town. Mother preferred to stay at
home with Socrates and have a little rest. She
gave Father the car keys and said, 'Drive carefully, Edward. Are you quite sure you want to?'

'Yes of course, don't worry,' said Father.

He was terribly proud when he went off with
the keys of the car, and Aurora was quite proud
as well. After all it was the first time she had
gone for a drive with Daddy. She hoped very
much that Nusse or Brit-Karen would be outside
so that they could see them.

But of course there was nobody there – yes,
there was, her friend, Knut. He was with some
other boys, and Aurora noticed that he opened

his eyes wide when Father got in and sat behind the steering-wheel.

Aurora crept into the back seat as usual, and Uncle Brande sat beside Father. Uncle Brande was one of those people who could look after a baby and make a cake and drive a car, even

though he didn't look as if he could do any of these things.

Father started the car and shot off like a bullet from a gun, for he wasn't used to this car. He had learnt to drive on quite a different one.

At that particular moment, Aurora thought that on the whole it didn't matter so much that Brit-Karen and Nusse weren't there. Father soon settled down and drove very carefully, and

even though there was an odd little jerk every
time he had to change gear, he was doing well.

He drove down the hill to the town, and when
they came to the busy streets, Uncle Brande
gave him some quiet words of advice. 'Move
over to your right a bit here. Now you can
take it nice and steady. Give a right hand signal,
and drive on to the second turning because the
other one is a one way street.'

'Yes,' said Father. Aurora thought that it
looked as if Daddy was clutching the wheel and
was a bit out of breath, but he was getting on
quite well all the same.

Father drove right down to where Uncle
Brande's bus was waiting.

'Thank you for all your help today, Brande,' he said. 'It was very good of you to come to us. I couldn't very well take Socrates with me to the driving test, could I?'

'No, of course not,' said Uncle Brande. 'You are sure you feel all right about driving home now, Edward? Take those streets down there, I think that will be your best way.'

'Yes,' said Father, 'and there are very clear road signs everywhere.'

'It seems silly for you to stand here waiting until the bus goes,' said Uncle Brande.

'We always stay with our guests until they are out of sight,' said Father.

Uncle Brande laughed so heartily that his bearded face shook as he sat there in the bus.

'I'm just going over the road to buy some tobacco,' said Father. 'You stay here, Aurora.'

As soon as Father had gone, Uncle Brande signalled to her and came to the door of the bus.

'Listen, Aurora,' he said. 'Maybe Daddy will feel a little, shall we say, unsure of himself when he has to drive all on his own now. Everybody is like that for the first few times, so it's nothing unusual. Just tell him to take it easy. If he suddenly forgets what to do, tell him to put on the hand brake and stop and switch off. Then say, "Now start off as you usually do" and he'll be all right again. Don't tell him I've said this. I think he did very well indeed, but I know what it can be like.'

'Mm,' said Aurora. 'Here comes Daddy.'

Father tossed a packet of tobacco to Uncle Brande. 'That's for the journey,' he said.

Now it was time for the bus to go, and Aurora and her father stood there until they couldn't see Uncle Brande any longer.

'Well, it's up to us now,' said Father. 'Come along, Aurora. I wish you could sit beside me but as you're a child you must sit behind.'

'I'm quite big,' said Aurora. 'If I sit on a cushion I'll look almost grown-up.'

'That won't do,' said Father, 'but you can watch out for the signs for me all the same.'

'All right,' said Aurora. She sat in the back seat and Father switched on the engine. It went all right even though the start was a bit jerky.

'Well,' said Father, 'in a way this is the very first time I've driven alone, for Uncle Brande kept telling me what to do, so I wasn't really managing on my own when we drove down.'

'I'm here,' said Aurora.

'Of course you are,' said Father, 'and that's fine, but I can't talk to you just now, because I've got enough to do to think about my driving.'

'Yes,' said Aurora. She could hardly speak, she was so anxious that Father should look round him properly.

She watched for the road signs, for she knew them nearly all, and suddenly she shouted, 'No, Daddy, you mustn't go down there, it says "No entry".'

'Thank you,' said Father. He had already driven a few yards down the street and now he stopped.

'Do you think I can back?' he asked. 'Is the road clear behind me?'

'No,' said Aurora. 'There's a lady walking right behind us.'

'I must wait then,' said Father.

'It's clear now,' said Aurora, 'but cars are coming along the other street.'

'We'll wait until we can see that it's clear there too,' said Father.

'Now it's clear both ways,' said Aurora.

Father looked out of the window and in the mirror, and then he was a little too eager and pressed so hard on the accelerator that the car shot backwards.

'Stop!' shouted Aurora. Father had almost run into the corner of a house, but he stopped in time and drove forward again and turned into the street correctly.

Luckily the street ran uphill and there was a car in front of him and one behind him so he could just go along with them. But at the top of the hill there was a crossroads with red and green lights, and just as Father was going over, of course the lights turned red and he had to stop.

'Just wait quietly,' muttered Father to himself, and pulled on the handbrake as he had been taught. He did something or other with the gears too, but Aurora didn't know much about that.

'Now we're going to do a hill start, Aurora,' he said. 'This can be tricky.'

He sounded quite confident and Aurora thought how clever he was.

'The light's green now, Daddy,' said Aurora.

'Yes,' said Father. 'Look, Aurora, I take the brake off and start at the same time.'

He pressed the accelerator, but something was wrong, for he ran backwards instead of forwards while the engine made a frightful noise.

'Stop! Brake, Daddy!' said Aurora.

The cars behind them hooted, and the one nearest to them hooted loudest, for although it was quite a big car it was afraid of getting Father's car on its bonnet. It got it on the bumper instead, and thanks to the fact that Father jammed the brakes on, there was only a little bump.

'Take it easy, Daddy,' said Aurora. 'Put on the handbrake and switch off the engine.'

'Yes,' said Father. He was so confused that he didn't even wonder how Aurora could tell him what to do so cleverly.

The other driver got out and glared at Father.

'What on earth do you think you're doing, man?' he said.

'It's my first time out,' said Father. 'I'm sorry, what shall I do?'

'Drive round that corner and then we can talk,' said the man. All of a sudden he wasn't angry any more, for he had seen from Father's expression that here was no road-hog, but a man who was scared out of his wits and must be handled gently.

He got into his car again, and Father said, 'Aurora! I've no idea what to do. I can't drive. I don't remember how to start.'

'Now, Daddy,' said Aurora, 'do just what you usually do. What do you do in your driving lesson when you start?'

'I switch on the ignition, let out the clutch, and put the car into first gear,' said Father. 'Ah, I hadn't got it properly in gear, that's why it rolled back. Now I understand.' He started again.

'The light's red,' said Aurora.

'Oh yes,' said Father. 'We must wait, but in any case I remember what to do now.'

'Just take it easy,' said Aurora.

'I don't know what would have happened if I hadn't had you with me,' said Father.

They turned into a little street and Father

drew up neatly beside the kerb. The big car behind him did the same.

'Now we must get out,' said Father.

Aurora realized that Father wanted her to be with him. She jumped out and quickly took his hand so that the man should understand that he couldn't do just what he liked, because she was watching. But she need not have been anxious, for the man who had looked so angry a few minutes ago, was now kindness itself. 'There's not much harm done,' he said. 'I got a fright when I saw you rolling back on me, but it was all right and it was a very good thing that you were able to brake at the last minute. Look here! I've only got a dent in the bumper, so shall we say a hundred kroner? Then it will be finished with and I shan't make any more fuss about it.'

A hundred kroner? Aurora stared at the man in dismay. That would buy a lot of dinners, she thought.

But Father said, 'That's quite all right. It was good of you to take it like that. I wasn't very proud of myself just then, I can tell you.'

'I'd like to see the fellow who doesn't do something crazy in the first few days after he's learnt to drive,' said the man. 'I backed into a fence the first time I went out.'

'That was kind of you,' said Father, whatever

he meant by that. But he was probably still a little confused.

He took out his wallet, and in it there were a few coins and a hundred kroner note.

'Here you are,' he said. 'Is everything all right now?'

'I'll give you a receipt,' said the man. 'Just take it easy in future!'

'I'm wondering whether I should leave the car here and fetch it later,' said Father.

'No,' said the man. 'That's the very thing you mustn't do. Get into your car and drive twice as far as you had meant to, and after that you'll be all right.'

'Thanks very much for that advice,' said Father.

'Otherwise, you see, you'll lose your nerve,' said the man, 'and then you'll never drive well again.'

He got into the big car and drove off, and left Aurora and her father sitting there.

'That was the housekeeping money, Aurora,' said Father. 'I shall have to try and find some evening work playing the piano to make it up again.'

Father sat in the car but didn't drive off. He sat and looked at all the knobs and thought of everything he had to remember, and he was nervous. Aurora could hear that in his voice.

'Now Daddy,' said Aurora, 'you must see that everything is in order and then you must start. Take off the brake and do what you usually do.'

'How on earth do you know all this?' said Father. 'Is it I or you who have been having driving lessons?'

'You,' said Aurora, 'but I'm pretending to be your driving instructor.'

'I see,' said Father. He smiled and did exactly as he had been taught. 'We won't go straight home,' he said, 'we'll drive round until I'm not nervous any longer.'

He drove along many streets and over difficult crossroads, and he and Aurora kept a careful look out, and finally he drove down to the quayside. Aurora looked at the boats and almost forgot that it was Daddy who was driving.

'Do you know, I'm enjoying it now,' said Father. 'I don't think I'll ever forget this first drive of mine.'

'Nor shall I,' said Aurora.

When at last they drew up in front of Block Z, Mother was standing on the balcony on the tenth floor and watching for them.

This time, both Brit-Karen and Nusse were outside and they came running up to the car. They stared at Father and said, 'Can you drive? We thought it was only Aurora's mummy who could.'

'Did you?' said Father. 'I think it's parked properly, Aurora, don't you?'

He walked round the car to see that the wheels were close in to the kerb and Knut came up and whispered to Aurora, 'He's forgotten to shut the windows.'

'Daddy,' said Aurora, 'I don't think we need to air the car any more now.'

'No, we don't,' said Father. He got in and fastened the windows and locked the car after him.

Then he sighed, just as if he were rather sorry to leave it.

'Do you think I could come out with you some time?' said Knut.

'Of course,' said Aurora.

'Come up with us and have some waffles,' said Father, 'there are heaps left.'

When they got upstairs, Mother said, 'My goodness, what a long time you've been! I've had a nap, and I've been waiting and waiting and I was almost certain that something had gone wrong. Are you both all right?' she said and looked hard at Aurora.

'Oh yes,' said Aurora.

'Shall I say we've had a slight mishap,' said Father. 'I'll tell you about it.'

Mother listened, and then she smiled and said, 'I drove straight into a kiosk the first time I took the car out.'

'You never told me that,' said Father.

'No, I didn't want to frighten you,' said Mother. 'Did you fetch your papers from the University?'

'Oh, I forgot!' said Father.

'So did I,' said Aurora.

'The worst of it is, I need them,' said Father.

'Let's have something to eat and then we'll all drive down there,' said Mother, 'Socrates and I would like to go with you. Do you want to come, Knut?'

'Yes please,' said Knut.

'Perhaps you had better go up and ask your mother first,' said Father.

'She isn't at home, so it doesn't matter where I am,' said Knut.

The drive didn't turn out quite as they had expected. Something very unusual happened . . .

4. Something About Mother

'WE are in a bit of a hurry so I think it will be best if you drive down, Marie,' said Father, 'and I'll drive back.'

'All right,' said Mother. Aurora thought she sounded rather relieved. Mother took the car keys and went down ahead of them, and when the others joined her she seemed to be walking round the car to see if it was undamaged. It wasn't, of course, because when it rolled back into the bumper of the other car, it had got a little dent itself.

'Oh well,' said Mother, 'I'll take it in to the garage tomorrow and get that dent removed. It's nothing much.'

They got in and Mother drove quickly into town. She had no trouble because she had done the journey a hundred times already and knew exactly where she had to stop and where she could go, and in no time at all they were outside the University.

While Father was inside, Knut and Aurora played in the forecourt. It was good to be a long way from Tiriltoppen, for down here Knut didn't mind playing with her *outside*. He wouldn't do that up at Tiriltoppen; he would only play with her *indoors*.

Father came back and now it was his turn to drive. It was then that something happened to Mother. Usually she was cheerful and good-tempered, and just rather quiet when she was tired. Now she suddenly became a quite different person before their very eyes. As soon as Father was going to start the car she said, 'No, no, you must take off the brake first, Edward. You didn't

give a signal when you moved off. Why in the world are you dawdling so? . . . You must keep up with the traffic, you know. Help! Keep to the right, or I'll jump out! . . . Put the brake on! No, go on, can't you see that the others are waiting? Oh my goodness, how you're racing the engine!'

Aurora could see that Father was clutching the steering-wheel hard, and suddenly it was just as though he had forgotten nearly everything he had learnt.

Then Aurora said, 'Just take it easy, Daddy, and do what you usually do.'

Mother looked astounded, and Father gave the ghost of a smile. Aurora could see that he wasn't clutching the wheel quite so hard any longer.

Mother didn't speak as loudly as she had done to begin with, but Socrates could hear from her voice that she was wrought up and so he got angry and began to yell. Poor Father, he thought that Socrates wasn't satisfied with his driving either.

Knut didn't say anything, just sat and looked out of the window, and Aurora patted her father's shoulder now and then and said, 'I think you are ever so clever, Daddy.'

They got home at last, and Father remembered to shut all the windows and lock the car properly, but he didn't look at all happy. He just picked up Socrates and carried him indoors while Mother walked round the car to see whether any harm had come to it.

'Good-bye,' said Knut, 'thank you for taking me.'

'Good-bye,' said Mother. Usually she would certainly have said that he could come in for a little while, but now all she said was 'Come along, Aurora.'

'All right,' said Aurora, but she didn't move from behind the car.

'I don't like you any more,' she said. 'Now Mummy gets so angry and Daddy is miserable, I don't like you any more. I don't think I ever want to ride in you again.'

Then she ran upstairs too. Home wasn't a very happy place that evening. If only everything could be as it used to be! Aurora sat and thought for a long time.

'We won't go out in the car tomorrow,' she said at last.

'I think I must have it for the office,' said Mother.

'Yes, but afterwards,' said Aurora, 'we won't go out in it. Can't we go to the wood instead?'

'By the way, Edward, who is it who lives in the wood and sends you waffles?' asked Mother.

'Perhaps we'll show Mummy our secret place,' said Father. 'I would like to go for a walk in the wood tomorrow, too.'

Aurora looked from Mummy to Daddy. They weren't quite their usual cheerful selves yet, but perhaps things were a little better. Not good enough, though.

Aurora didn't want anything to eat, she just went to bed. In the bedroom, Socrates was screaming. It was so silly. She was lying here and feeling miserable, and in there he was miserable too.

'Can't Socrates come in to me?' she asked.

'Yes, why not?' said Father. 'Mummy, shall we move his cot into Aurora's room? We've thought about putting him in there for a long time.'

'All right,' said Mother. She was almost herself again now, and when she and Father lifted Socrates' bed, they began to laugh and talk together as they usually did.

Socrates calmed down at once. No more angry voices, no angry Socrates either.

'Hallo, Socrates,' said Aurora, 'you're going to stay with me now.'

Socrates lay for a while thinking about it. He wondered whether he had made a mistake or whether it really was true that Aurora was in the same room with him. 'D-ah!' he said.

'Yes,' said Aurora, 'I'm here. Good night, Socrates.' Socrates yawned and said 'dah' once more, and Aurora was very glad that he was with her. It was so safe and comfortable when Socrates lay there and she could hear him breathing . . .

Next morning everything was back to normal. Father was up early and had done the children's washing before Mother had her breakfast, and Mother sat there eating and reading the newspaper, and Father brought her lunch-packet and gave her a good-bye hug, and Aurora waved.

'I think I shall do a lot of work today,' said Father. 'It will be good to get on with my history again. I've promised myself to have my thesis ready by the autumn in any case. It's a very good thing that the car is away all the morning, then I don't have to think about it.'

'I don't ever want to go out in the car again,' said Aurora.

'What's that you're saying?' said Father in dismay.

'No, because Mummy's not like she usually is.'

'Oh,' said Father. 'You're thinking about yesterday, aren't you? Now listen to me. Up to now, this car has only been Mummy's. She has driven it every single day. Often when she has felt tired and depressed, it has brought her safely home. She knows all about it, and just how to handle it to get the best out of it, and so it was terrible for her to sit beside me and watch me drive. So she's not coming out with me again until I'm a bit better.'

'I think you were good,' said Aurora.

'Yes, when you and I are alone perhaps I am a bit better, except when I rolled back into that other car, because you're so good at making me think. We must practise, Aurora, and when we are much more sure of ourselves we can ask Mummy to go out with us.'

'Yes,' said Aurora, 'but not today because today we're going to the wood. You promised.'

'Yes,' said Father, 'I did.'

Mother didn't have an afternoon nap that day. They just put on slacks and sweaters and then set off.

All four of them were happy because they were going for a walk.

Socrates sat in the pram and waved to the other babies who were being pushed along to the wood.

'What a pity we don't do this every day,' said Mother. 'Was this what you wanted to show me?'

'Not exactly,' said Father, 'but it's part of it. It's the best thing about Tiriltoppen that we have the wood so close to us.'

'I'm sure there are foxes here,' said Mother, 'and hares.'

'And adders too,' said Aurora, 'Knut told me so.'

'Mm,' said Mother, 'and lots of birds as well.'

'And mice,' said Aurora, 'but no bears.'

'We'll soon be there now,' Father whispered to Aurora. He didn't say any more because he wanted Mother to discover it for herself . . .

And there was the little house in the middle of the wood, with the birch tree in the yard and the cowshed and the woodshed and the little shed with the heart-shaped hole in the door.

'Oh, how lovely!' said Mother. 'Just look at it! To think that there's a house here, right in the middle of the wood.'

'That's what our secret was,' said Aurora. 'Daddy and I found it on Christmas Eve.'

'Yes, we did,' said Father. 'Isn't it lovely and peaceful here?'

'Indeed it is,' said Mother. 'Do you think we can go a little closer?'

'Of course we can,' said Father. 'We can go and say hallo to the people who live here.'

'Can we really?' asked Mother.

'Certainly,' said Father. They walked slowly forward, and Mother drew a deep breath and said, 'How pretty it is and how quiet!'

Just as she said that, it wasn't quiet any longer.

There was a loud burst of music.

It wasn't the kind of music that Father played, or the kind that the band played in the street either.

'It can't be the radio,' said Father.

'No,' said Mother. They looked at each other, and Mother looked at Socrates for he was sitting in his pram and rocking in time with the music, and over there in the cowshed it sounded as if someone was playing by himself.

'You're a fine pair,' said Mother. 'Is this what you call quiet and peaceful?' But she was laughing delightedly. 'I can see some instruments shining in there.'

Now the music stopped, and out of the door came Gran with a big drum strapped to her chest. 'You're welcome,' she said.

58

'Good heavens,' said Father, 'have you got a whole orchestra?'

'Yes, there are quite a lot of us,' said Gran. 'Today it's a practice for Ole Alexander's Woody Woody Band – they have to have a funny name like that or they don't catch on. They play for dances and earn a bit of money so they can go and learn more music. On Mondays they play the classical stuff and on Fridays their dad has a

59

practice with the lorry-drivers' band. Come in, do.'

'We don't want to interrupt,' said Mother.

'You won't do that,' said Gran. 'Just you come in, now. We're going to play one more tune and then we have a rest. Socrates had better stay outside though, it's a bit too noisy for him.'

A little black and brown dog came rushing out of the house.

'That's Stove-pipe,' said Gran. 'He likes visitors although he sounds rather fierce.'

Mother and Father and Aurora peeped inside. There sat a man and a woman and certainly eight children, or were there nine?

5. Father Springs a Surprise

THEY were going to have a break now, and Gran pointed out one after the other the people who were sitting or standing about inside the house. 'This is Mother, and that's Father, and then we have Maren, Martin, Marte, Mads, Mona, Milly, Mina and Little Morten, though he's not so little any longer for he goes to school, and then there's Ole Alexander but he doesn't belong to the family. He's a friend of ours and lives up at Tiriltoppen.'

'He's the boy who took Puff away that time,' Aurora whispered to her father.

'It's only the bigger ones who play in the dance band,' said Gran, 'but they're all in the band at Tiriltoppen.'

Aurora looked very hard at the boy who was called Little Morten, for he played a little drum and that seemed to be great fun.

'They let Morten and me practise with them here at home,' said Gran, 'but we don't go with them when they play somewhere else, and they don't take the youngest girl either.'

The mother of the family brought in coffee, and Gran said to the children 'Now you can go outside for ten minutes, or let's say a quarter of an hour as we have visitors.'

The older children smiled, but they sauntered off, and the little ones hopped and skipped and looked at Aurora as they went. Aurora looked at them but she wasn't quite brave enough to go outside with them at once. They were a bit bigger than she was, too.

But when Mother had drunk her coffee, she said, 'Is it true that you've got cows here?'

'We've got one cow at any rate,' said the

children's mother. 'Perhaps you would like to go with me and see Rosie.'

'Oh yes,' said Aurora. 'You come too, Mummy.'

Father stayed indoors and sat talking to Gran and the children's father. They had a pleasant chat, and Father remembered that he mustn't say that Gran was taking driving lessons because that was her secret.

'How do you come to know this gentleman, Gran?' asked the children's father.

'I met him in the supermarket up at Tiril-toppen,' said Gran. 'We ground our coffee together . . . and now you've passed your driving test, so I heard Aurora say. I suppose you'll be driving all the time now.'

'No,' said Father, and his face grew serious. 'At first I was very proud and happy and thought I knew what I was doing, but now it seems much more difficult. I've lost confidence in myself, and I do such a lot of silly things, especially when my wife is with me. She has driven for a long time, and of course she thinks it's dreadful to watch me driving. I haven't driven at all today.'

'When did you pass your test?' asked the children's father.

'Yesterday,' said Father.

Gran looked at Father, and then she began to whisper, and the children's father nodded, and then he began to whisper too, and in the end Father looked quite cheerful. They were such kind people.

'I could help you by writing out music for you if there is anything you need for the orchestra,' said Father. 'I know a bit about it. I play the piano.'

'That's fine,' said Gran. 'Now you had better go out to the cowshed too, in case they think we've been up to something, and of course we have been, but nobody must know about it.'

They went into the cowshed, and Father saw the cow called Rosie.

Rosie was Gran's cow, and she had a son. He was quite big now, but even so he was called Little Bull.

'Don't you think you will soon have to change his name?' said Father.

'Oh no,' said Gran. 'He may be big, but he's really like a little child. He's frightened of his mother and does everything she wants.'

'I see,' said Father. 'Do you let him out in the summer?'

'Yes, he's been wandering about today,' said Gran, 'but we keep him in on Sundays, he's so scared of people.'

'Yes,' said Father. Perhaps he thought that the people might be scared of Little Bull, but he didn't say so.

At the back of the shed, behind some netting, sat five hens with their heads tucked into their feathers, and when they came out into the yard again, Stove-pipe was lying quietly beside Socrates' pram, keeping guard.

'Well, we must be getting home,' said Father. 'Thank you so much.'

'I always think it's so nice to have visitors,' said Gran.

Father was so cheerful on the way home that Aurora wondered what he was thinking about, but he didn't say anything.

After a few days, Mother began to wonder too, for Father disappeared every evening. He always asked whether Mother was going to be at home, and whether she minded if he went out because he had something important to do. Mother said it was quite all right, because Father had done all his household jobs, and everything was tidy in the kitchen, and he had worked hard and studied a great deal of history in the middle of the day.

The car was standing outside, but Father didn't look at it once. Aurora thought this was odd. He had struggled to learn to drive and now it seemed as if he wasn't thinking about the car at all.

Mother asked too, 'Aren't you going to take the car out for a little while, Edward? You must keep in practice, you know.'

It was just as if Block Z had eyes, for it wasn't long before one person after another came up to Aurora and said, 'Didn't your daddy learn to drive? Doesn't he ever use the car?'

'He's so busy with his history,' said Aurora.

It must have been a queer sort of history that Father was studying, for when he came home in the evening he had oil on his hands and his face wasn't very clean. He hurried into the bathroom immediately and washed so that Mother shouldn't notice anything.

If it was fine in the afternoon, most people came out of the block and sat on the grass out-

66

side. They brought coffee and a rug with them, and sat and enjoyed themselves while the children ran about.

One day when the sun was shining and Mother and Father and Socrates and Aurora were sitting there, Mother said, 'Are you going to leave us today too, Edward?'

'No, I don't think so,' said Father. 'I must spend a bit of time at home now.'

There were a lot of people outside today, nearly everyone they knew in the block.

Nusse and her parents were there, and Brit-Karen and her father and mother, and Knut and the lady who lived two floors below them, the one on whose head a little glove had fallen when Father aired the woollens.

Some of the men were washing their cars. Father puffed at his pipe, and played with Aurora, and looked into the distance.

Then suddenly the loud drone of an engine was heard, and two lorries arrived. The first was a little red truck, and in the driver's seat sat the father of the eight children from the house in the wood. Their mother was beside him, and in the back were Gran and the youngest children.

Behind the little red truck came a big lorry, and in the back stood Ole Alexander and the older children from the house in the wood, and they were playing their instruments.

67

All the children from the block gathered round them, and the grown-ups sat and smiled and beat time, and thought what fun it was to have music with their coffee.

When they had finished playing, the children's father got out of the truck and shouted, 'Is your daddy here, Aurora?'

'Yes,' said Aurora. 'He's sitting over there on the grass, smoking his pipe.'

'That's good,' he said. 'We've got to drive these youngsters into town because they are to play at a club today, and it's difficult for the other driver to take them because it's his little boy's fourth birthday and he's promised to be at home.'

'Oh,' said Aurora. She didn't really know what he was getting at.

'So we wondered if your daddy would drive the lorry for him,' he went on.

Aurora opened her mouth but she didn't say anything, she just ran across the grass and shouted, 'Daddy, Daddy, he's asking if you can drive the big lorry because the other man has got to go to a birthday party.'

Mother laughed and shook her head. 'Don't be silly,' she said. 'You know Daddy can't do it.'

But Father just got up calmly and picked up the jacket that he had laid on the grass.

'That will be quite all right,' he said.

68

The other driver climbed down from his high
cab and said, 'Edward, can you back up that
narrow road there and turn, because the others
want to go in front of you. They can't see anything if they are behind you.'

'Certainly,' said Father. He got in. 'See if the

road's clear, will you?' he said. 'There are so
many children running about.'

He pushed his cap back and looked carefully
round him, and backed the heavy lorry up the
narrow road. Then he waited until the truck had
turned, waved to Mother and the others and
drove off, and as he drove the band played again.

Aurora thought they seemed to be playing

for Daddy, and that is just what they were doing.

Mother sat quite still. 'Oh,' she said, 'and I who . . . Oh, goodness me . . . Haven't we got an exciting Daddy, Aurora?'

'Yes, we have,' answered Aurora.

'We think your daddy can drive all right,' said Nusse.

'I think so too,' said Brit-Karen, 'and wasn't it fun when they played!'

'Yes,' said Mother, 'it was.' She took Aurora and Socrates upstairs, and when Socrates was changed and fed, she and Aurora sat down to wait for Father. They had laid a specially good supper but they didn't want to eat it until he came. At last they heard a heavy lorry making its way up the hill.

'There he is!' shouted Aurora.

The lorry stopped down below, and the other driver came back and took it over. Father touched his cap smartly and seemed to be thanking him for the loan, and then he went into the block.

He certainly didn't say no to the nice supper that Mother and Aurora had prepared for him. 'Edward,' said Mother, 'I hardly know what to say. Was I awful that time I went out with you?'

'You were, rather,' said Father, 'but I think I understand how you felt, and that was why I was determined to go on until you could really trust my driving.'

'I do now,' said Mother.

Father was happy and contented again, and the funny thing was that most people in the block were aware that he was good at playing the piano and knew a tremendous amount of history, but in their eyes the fact that he had learnt to drive a lorry outshone everything else; and Father thought so too.

One evening he sat writing out a lot of music.

'What are you up to now?' asked Mother.

'I'm writing out a march for the lorry-drivers' band,' said Father.

'Do you belong to that?' asked Mother.

'I am an honorary member,' said Father, smiling.

6. Summer at Tiriltoppen

BLOCK Z was a strange place in the summer. Father called it their private residence, for it seemed as if only Aurora and Mother and Father and Socrates were still there. Well, there were some other people, but not very many.

Father wasn't going to have a summer holiday, because he had to do a great deal of reading about the Ancient Greeks and write something called a thesis, and the thesis must be finished by the autumn. Father sat up late every single night and was terribly tired the next day, and he went on reading in the morning when he wasn't washing

up or seeing to Socrates or cooking the dinner.

Mother put off her summer holiday until the autumn too, so that she could have it at the same time as Father, and if anyone asked Aurora why she hadn't gone away, she said, 'This year I'm putting off my summer holiday until the autumn.

After that there was nothing more to say. As a matter of fact, Aurora and Socrates should have gone to stay with their own Granny that summer, but Granny wasn't well and had got something called sciatica, so she couldn't have visitors. But it didn't matter very much because Block Z was so strange and exciting in the summer.

Sometimes when Aurora walked down the long corridor, it was almost uncanny, for there wasn't a sound to be heard. If a door suddenly slammed it was more uncanny still, for then the sound seemed louder than usual.

Nusse was staying with her aunt in the country, Brit-Karen had gone camping, and Knut was at a children's holiday camp, but Nusse's mother was at home because she had taken a job for the summer and was out every evening, running round with plates and dishes in a restaurant, as she had explained to Aurora.

Sometimes when it was raining and Socrates was asleep and Father was reading, Aurora went up to see her because she had got to know her quite well.

One day she was making jam when Aurora arrived. There was a lovely smell of raspberries and strawberries in the kitchen, and a big pan full of jam stood on the stove. On the work-top

were rows of clean, empty jars and there were some more in the oven. These were warm, and now she took them out one at a time and filled them with the boiling jam and quickly put a cover on them.

She was very quick and deft and Aurora enjoyed watching her. Neither of them spoke much, but Nusse's mother's hands seemed to be saying a whole lot of things. 'That's *that* jar finished, and that's *that* one, and we shall be glad of this in the winter. Oh, the outside of this one is rather sticky. We'll wipe it with a hot cloth, so.'

Finally there were ten full jars on the work-top. There was still a little jam left in the pan, and this was scraped out and given to Aurora to eat. It was delicious. Aurora ate as slowly as she could so that she could be quite sure that she was really getting the full taste of it.

'We'll leave them like this until tomorrow,' said Nusse's mother, 'and then we'll put them down in the cellar. Come up here tomorrow, Aurora, and perhaps you can help me to carry them.'

'Yes, I'd like to,' said Aurora.

She ran upstairs the next morning, and was allowed to carry a basket with two jars of jam in it. Nusse's mother managed to take all the others because she had two shopping bags and put four jars in each. They took the lift down to the base-ment and went along the long, cold passage. If it was quiet elsewhere in the building it was much quieter here. Quiet and cold.

'I'm very glad you're with me,' said Nusse's mother. 'I don't like being alone here.'

'Is it dangerous, then?' asked Aurora.

'No, but it's so quiet.'

She unlocked the store cupboard, and there were rows and rows of jars of jam and bottles of fruit juice.

'Oh, what a lot of jam you've got!' said Aurora.

'Yes, I get the fruit from my husband's sister who lives in the country,' said Nusse's mother. 'Nusse is staying with her now.'

'I see,' said Aurora. She couldn't stop looking at all the jars that were lined up on the shelves.

That day, Aurora spoke seriously to her father. He was cooking the dinner so it was all right to talk to him then.

'How much jam have we got in the cellar?' asked Aurora.

'Jam?' said Father, and looked as if he didn't know what it was.

'Yes, for the winter,' said Aurora. 'Nusse's Mummy has a whole lot already, and she's going to have a lot more.'

'Oh yes, jam for the winter, in jars, you mean. I'm afraid we've forgotten all about it. We absolutely must have some! I remember how good it used to smell when my mother made it at home, the only thing was that so many wasps always came in.'

'We can shut the window,' said Aurora.

'But fruit is dear to buy, Aurora,' said Father, 'and we haven't so much as a single bush here.'

He and Aurora looked out of the window to make sure. In front of the block there was a very big lawn but no bushes – yes, in one corner at the far end there were three small bushes but they were for ornament, and were not fruit bushes.

'There could have been red and blackcurrants all round the lawn,' said Father, 'and cherry and apple and plum trees in the middle. Then there would have been a little fruit for everyone. I shall propose that at the next general meeting of the block.'

'Oh yes,' said Aurora. 'If only all the blocks had them!'

'Yes,' said Father. 'If only the whole of Tiriltoppen had red and blackcurrant bushes in front of the blocks of flats!'

He got so excited that he fetched paper and pencil and drew Block Z with all the bushes and trees on the lawn. It looked fine, and Aurora felt her mouth watering at the thought of all that fruit. She stood and looked at it for a long time and then she said, 'But it won't be ready for the winter, will it, Daddy?'

'No,' said Father, 'that's true. We haven't any bushes yet and we've hardly any money, and what we have we must spend on food. I'm afraid.'

'We could go to the wood,' said Aurora. 'I saw some people with pails yesterday who had been picking bilberries.'

'We'll do that tomorrow,' said Father. 'But don't tell Mummy. It will be a big surprise for her if the two of us find some fruit and make jam.'

The next day, Father and Aurora and Socrates went off to the wood. Socrates didn't quite understand what was going on but he loved being in the wood. He was nearly a year old now, and had begun to walk a little. He fell down from time to time, but he managed to keep upright for quite a long while, provided he had something to hold in his hand. It might be a piece of paper, or something of that sort. Today he was holding a tiny little bilberry leaf and he seemed to think this would support him, but he fell down all the same and lost the little leaf.

'You shall have another one,' said Father and bent over a little bilberry twig to pick a leaf for his little boy.

Socrates looked as if he couldn't believe his ears. He would never have thought that Father could suggest anything so silly. So Aurora and Father had to get down on all fours and try to find just the very leaf that he had had before.

Aurora found it, and Socrates was happy once more. He took a few quick little steps forward and was going quite fast before he fell down again. But this time, fortunately, he clutched his bilberry leaf in both hands. Then he got up and staggered on. He kept going until he tumbled into some heather and just lay there.

Father lowered the back of the push-chair so that Socrates could lie there instead and have a little rest. But tired as he was, he glared at Father and complained as loudly as he could.

'Would you like a bilberry?' said Aurora and popped a lovely big fat berry into his mouth.

Socrates tasted it and his eyes grew round and shining, it was so delicious. He ate it slowly, and when at last he had finished it he fell asleep, and Father and Aurora could really begin to pick. They had brought two pails and a large yellow plastic bucket with them.

'What would you sooner pick, bilberries or raspberries?' asked Father.

'Bilberries, I think,' said Aurora, 'because they are all over the place.'

'I'm going up that slope to see if I can find any raspberries,' said Father. 'Promise me to look where you're going so that you don't disturb any adders.'

'If the adder sees me coming, will he come after me?'

'Of course not,' said Father, 'but if you tread on him it won't make any difference to him that you didn't mean it.'

'No,' said Aurora. She stamped her feet so that the adder could hear her coming.

When Father had climbed some way up the slope, she began to talk to the adder too, just to be on the safe side. She couldn't see him, but she might as well speak to him in case he was somewhere near.

'I'm not dangerous,' she said, 'I'm quite small although I seem big to you.'

There was one little bilberry rolling round in her pail now. 'That's the first,' said Aurora.

A little farther on there were so many berries that she could just squat down and pick and pick.

Once she tried to count the berries, but they all got mixed up and kept rolling about.

'Well, Aurora, have you got a lot?' shouted Father. I'm sure there are a hundred,' said Aurora, 'but it doesn't look like it.'

'I shall soon have half a pail full,' said Father. 'Raspberries are so big that you can pick them more quickly, but it's not easy to walk up here so I'm glad you're stopping among the bilberries.'

Aurora and Father went on picking and hardly spoke.

Suddenly Aurora thought she heard a strange noise coming from amongst the trees. It was some way away, but there was Father hurrying down the slope.

'Well, I think we've got enough now, Aurora,' he said. 'We have to make the jam and then get the dinner ready before Mummy comes.'

He was walking very fast, and now and then he looked back at the slope.

'Do adders make a noise?' asked Aurora.

'No,' said Father. 'Look, you take the pail and I'll take the push-chair and we'll run.'

When they had run a little way, Aurora looked back. Just where they had been, a large animal stood plunging its head into the bilberries, and then shaking it so that heather and bilberries were scattered all around.

'It's Gran's Little Bull,' said Aurora softly.

'Yes, so it is,' said Father. 'Gran said it was scared of people so I thought we had better go in case it should be frightened.'

A little boy came running up. He gave Little Bull a slap on the rump and said, 'You must go home now. I told you not to stay by yourself. Go to your mother at once.'

'That was the boy who played the little drum,' whispered Aurora. 'He's called Morten, you remember.'

'Well, well,' said Father. 'Now we must hurry, Aurora.'

Father had half a small bucket of fruit and Aurora had a quarter, almost, and now they were going to make jam.

When they were in the kitchen and had found a big preserving pan, Father said, 'Perhaps we had better put them together, it will make more.'

'Yes,' said Aurora. So the raspberries and the bilberries were put in the same pan, and soon there was the same delicious smell of jam as there had been in Nusse's mother's kitchen.

'Have you put the sugar in?' asked Aurora.

'Yes,' said Father, 'and it's boiled now.'

'Put it in the jar while it's hot, and then it will set,' said Aurora.

'Yes,' said Father. He took a ladle full and poured it into the jar.

'Crack!' went the jar and broke, and the jam splashed on to the walls, the floor, the work-top and the stove.

Luckily Socrates was in his play-pen, and Aurora didn't get any of the hot jam on her either.

'The jar should have been warmed first,' said Aurora.

'Yes,' said Father. He found another jar. First he poured in some hot water, and emptied it out again, and then he put only a very little jam in the bottom of the jar and swilled it round so that the jar could get used to the boiling jam, and then he went on adding a little more until the jar was quite full.

It wasn't big, but it had a proper lid and looked quite all right. Aurora was allowed to scrape out what was left in the pan, and then she and Father got down on the floor and washed off all the splashes with hot water and soap, and then Father cooked the dinner. They were both rather tired when Mother came home.

'Oh, what a lovely smell!' she said. 'It smells just as it did at home when I was a little girl and my mother had been making jam.'

'Would you like to look?' said Aurora.

She brought in the jar. It was cool now, and Father had stuck on a label.

'Bilberry and raspberry,' Mother read out. 'Oh, when shall we eat it, do you think? On a birthday or on Christmas Eve?'

'On a happy day in any case,' said Father.

Mother and Aurora and Socrates and Father all had to go down to put the jar in the cellar. It was placed in the middle of a shelf. There it stood in solitary state, and although it wasn't so very big, it was good to think that they had it.

7. The Post

ON the ground floor of Aurora's block, just inside the door, was a wall covered with green letter-boxes. They were there so that the postman wouldn't have to run up all the stairs to deliver letters.

It was Aurora's regular job to fetch the post. To start with it had been quite fun, but now she had almost begun to dread it, for many times recently there had been something that Father wasn't pleased to get. Once there had been a letter from something called the Tax Office which said straight out that they didn't believe what Father had told them some time ago. What Father had written was that he had earned five hundred kroner in one year, and he had earned that by playing the piano at some parties, and otherwise he had earned nothing because he had been sitting at home reading history, which had given him much pleasure but no money, as he said, and then he had done the washing-up every day of the year, which was something like a thousand washings-up for there were at least two a day, and he couldn't remember how many nappies he had washed, but Socrates had got up to six a day which came to something like two

thousand four hundred and ninety – not count-
ing all the other small garments he had washed,
and not to mention everything he had washed
down in the laundry-room – and he had boiled
three thousand and sixty potatoes, although he
frequently cooked spaghetti or rice instead for it
was often quite an undertaking to do potatoes,
but for all this he hadn't earned a penny.

Only today, Father had said before she went
to fetch the post, 'Now, Aurora, be a good girl
and don't bring us any bills today, because
Mummy won't get paid for three days and we
have one krone and forty øre – no, I'm sorry, I've
found another fifty øre. We have one krone and
ninety øre, and besides that we have four litres
of milk, and a big bag of porridge oats, and a
few tins, and some potatoes, so you needn't be
afraid that you won't get anything to eat, but no
bills, please.'

'All right then,' said Aurora. 'If there are any,
shall I just throw them away?'

She looked so worried that Father laughed and
said, 'No, my child, bring the lot and we'll find a
good place to hide them until we've got some
money in the house again.'

Aurora walked all the way downstairs for then
she could pretend that there was something nice
in the letter-box.

She was holding the key. It was very tiny and

had to be hung on a string in order to be seen. Now she swung it quickly round and round so that it looked like a wheel in the air. The wheel swung down the stairs until she reached the ground floor.

Aurora stood on tiptoe and unlocked the

letter-box, and there were two things in it. There was a loose sheet of paper with green letters on it and green lines and black numbers. That was the electric light bill. Aurora knew because she had seen one before.

The other, fortunately, was a letter – quite an ordinary letter and not the shiny kind with a transparent window in front which often meant something unpleasant.

It looked rather like one of Granny's letters. If only it were! If only it were so nice that Daddy would almost forget about the other one! Aurora wondered whether she should hide the electric light bill until they had some money, but perhaps that wouldn't be such a good idea, for supposing she were to hide it so well that she couldn't find it again herself, and then it wouldn't be paid and the light would be cut off, Daddy had said so.

No, it would be better for him to get it, but perhaps he could have Granny's letter first, that would please him.

No, Aurora changed her mind. He should have the nasty one first and the nice one afterwards.

She ran along her own corridor, opened the door which stood ajar, and went straight into Father. 'You must have the worst one first,' she said.

'Thank you very much,' said Father. 'Ah, the electricity bill, but that's all right because luckily it doesn't have to be paid for a long time. Put it in the grey box with "Unanswered" on it, it's on the bookcase.'

'And there's a letter as well,' said Aurora.

'Hm, it's from Mother,' said Father. 'Now we shall hear how her sciatica is. "My dear boy" . . .'

'Is it to Socrates?' asked Aurora.

'No, "my dear boy" is me,' said Father.

'Oh yes,' said Aurora.

'Well then, "My dear boy. How are you getting on in this summer heat? Is it necessary for you to do so much reading now? I think you should soon take a little holiday, perhaps a trip to the mountains would do you good. I can't have you all here because I'm still not quite well, but I'm much better so I'm on the right road. Now listen: could you do me a favour? I lie in bed reading the newspaper every morning and there's so much in it about the sales, with dresses and blouses and that kind of thing at cheaper prices. So, Edward, as you are quite free in the morning, I thought I could ask you if you would go to the sales for me and buy me a dress for the autumn, and a blouse for best, and perhaps a little scarf. I should really have asked Marie to do it, but she's so busy, poor girl, with the office and all of you, so I know how difficult it is for her.

I enclose a cheque for two hundred and fifty kroner. Spend a hundred and fifty for me, and with the other hundred buy something in the sales for Aurora and Socrates. There must be plenty of things they need. I hope the three of you will enjoy the outing. I thought it would do you good, too, my boy, to have a trip to town and

not just sit there poring over those Ancient
Greeks of yours. Give my love to Marie and the
children.

P.S. Measure the dress against yourself because

we're about the same size although you are a bit
taller".'

Father read it aloud once, and then he read it
to himself to be quite sure what it said.

Then he sat for some while with a queer
expression on his face.

At length he said, 'We must get on with this, Aurora. I haven't time but it can't be helped, I must do it all the same. We'll start as soon as Socrates wakes up.'

When Socrates had woken from his morning nap, he was in high spirits. At first he was a little put out because he couldn't quite remember who and where he was, but as soon as he had come to himself he was so lively that there was no holding him.

Aurora and her father realized this during the tram-ride into town. Father was glad when it was over. So was Aurora, and down in the town Socrates had so much to look at that he sat quietly in his push-chair.

'We'll go to a big store,' said Father, 'because we can get everything we want in one place and soon be finished, and then we can walk round and amuse ourselves afterwards.'

Father found a store, but when he went in he was a little bewildered because it was so crowded, there were so many people talking, and they had turned on some kind of music as well, to make sure that nobody could think clearly.

Socrates thought it was lovely, such a lot of lights in the ceiling and so many new things to pull down if only he could get out of the push-chair. Well, he could wait a little while.

Aurora was gazing at something else, for right

in front of her was a white horse with a red saddle, not a real horse but a big toy horse, and a little boy went and sat on it and then his mother put fifty øre in the horse and it began to move up

and down. The boy held on tight and it looked as if he was really riding.

'Come along now, Aurora,' said Father. 'We must go up to the next floor. I think I'll buy

Mother's dress and blouse first, and then we'll get your things afterwards.'

Aurora just looked at the horse.

Father glanced at the lift. It was full of people, so he looked at the stairs. It wouldn't be exactly easy to take the push-chair up there. He looked at Aurora again, and then he said, 'Perhaps you'd like to stay here with Socrates and wait for me while I go up to the next floor and get the things for Mother. I'll be quick.'

'All right,' said Aurora. She was very pleased that she was going to stay there.

Father went off, and Aurora held the push-chair and looked at the horse. It wasn't moving up and down quite so fast any longer, it went slower and slower until finally the little boy sat there quite still.

'Let me have another go!' he said to his mother. 'Just one more go, please!'

'Well, all right then,' she said, 'but after that, you must promise to come at once.'

She put in another coin. The boy began to leap and jump again. Aurora had to smile, it looked such fun.

At last his second turn was finished too.

'It's all right to sit on it, you don't have to pay for that,' he said to his mother.

'No,' she said, 'but you must come along now. I'm sure this little girl wants to have a go.' She took the boy's hand and went off with him, and Aurora was left alone in front of the horse. She was still holding the push-chair with one hand and with the other she cautiously patted the horse.

What was it that boy had said? It's all right to sit on it, you don't have to pay for that. Was that true? Aurora hadn't fifty øre and Father had used all his loose change, as well as a season ticket, on the tram. He had said that he had a hundred kroner to buy clothes with for her and Socrates, and perhaps he might have to take a little of it for the tram home and for a few other odds and ends, but he certainly didn't mean such things as that horse. Perhaps she could just stand beside it for a while.

The stirrup was dangling right in front of her eyes.

'I'll help you up, little girl,' said a man's voice, and with that he lifted her up and sat her down on the horse. He must have seen her standing there patting it, and perhaps he had thought that she couldn't manage to get on by herself.

'Shall we put in fifty øre?' he said.

Aurora shook her head. 'I haven't got it,' she said, 'but I think it's fun just sitting here.'

'Well, I must get on,' said the man. 'I've just come out in my lunch-break and thought of buying a shirt or two. You look fine sitting up there. Is it all right if I put fifty øre in for you?'

Aurora nodded. The man waited until the horse began to move. Then he waved and went off.

There sat Aurora. She held on tight and the horse walked. No, it didn't walk; it jumped and galloped, and Aurora was out for her first ride.

She was enjoying herself so much that she almost forgot Socrates, but suddenly she thought that she ought to try and wave to him, even though she must hold on tight. Then she saw that Socrates had scrambled out of the push-chair and was beginning to trot away.

Socrates knew nothing about horses, but he was very much concerned with trying out everything and seeing the world, and his fingers curled with pleasure at the idea of all they had to explore. But then he fell down, for he had nothing to hold on to, not even a bilberry leaf.

However, he soon put that right, for there lay a heap of handkerchiefs in a box. Socrates quickly made for this heap and found a pretty little silk handkerchief. He held it up and toddled off.

'Socrates, Socrates!' shouted Aurora. But the horse trotted and jumped and creaked, and people were talking to each other. Nobody noticed that she was calling to him.

Yes, Socrates did. He beamed at her and went

faster, for it was such fun to run away from her when she wanted to catch him.

But Aurora couldn't run after her brother. She had to wait until the horse stopped, and although she had been afraid that the ride would be much too short, she now found it was too long.

Meanwhile Father was on the first floor looking at rows and rows of dresses. Up here, the shop assistants who were packing parcels were terribly busy. In the fitting-rooms there was a buzz of conversation, and voices calling, and the saleswomen were rushing to and fro. Of course they saw Father standing there, but they thought that maybe his wife was in one of the fitting-rooms and he was waiting for her. But at last he lost patience and said, 'Is there anyone who can help me? Quickly?'

'Do you want something?' said one of the assistants. 'I thought you were just waiting for someone who was trying on a dress. Can we find something for your wife, perhaps?'

'No, for my mother,' said Father.

'What size?' said the assistant.

'Mine,' said Father. 'She is about as big as I am, not quite as tall, and perhaps a little thinner.'

'Would it be for a party or . . .?'

'For autumn,' said Father.

'Maybe something in black or brown, then,' said the assistant.

'Why?' asked Father.

'I understood it was for your mother,' said the assistant.

'Yes,' said Father. 'She likes white, pale blue, dark blue, red, and pale green.' The moment he had said this he caught sight of a pale blue dress. He took it from the row and held it against himself, but it was terribly short, for his trouser legs looked very long under the hem of the skirt.

Then the voice of a loudspeaker rang through the shop. 'A little boy has lost his mother. He can be fetched from the office. There is a display of boys' clothes on the second floor.'

Father thought no more about it, but suddenly he seemed to hear someone calling, 'Daddy! Daddy!'

Aurora had run all round the ground floor where she had seen Socrates disappear. She had called to him, but it seemed impossible to make herself heard in the midst of all those people.

Socrates had heard, of course, but he thought it was a fine game not to let himself be caught for a bit, so he made off as quickly as he could and didn't knock over anything much, but at last he was seized by a shop assistant.

Aurora didn't know this. She ran round one counter after another calling, 'Socrates! Socrates!'

'Are you looking for your dog?' asked a shop assistant.

'No,' said an elderly lady who was looking at the jewellery. 'Don't you know that Socrates was a Greek? He was extremely wise and lived over two thousand years ago. He's no dog, you can be sure!'

'No, he's a person,' said Aurora, 'and he's alive now. He's a year old.'

There were the stairs. She ran up them. 'Daddy! Daddy!'

There stood Father, holding a pale blue dress in front of him. He was so startled that he dropped it.

'Daddy, Socrates has gone!' shrieked Aurora. Tears rolled down her cheeks and she tugged at his arms.

'Gone?' said Father.

'Yes. I was sitting on the horse,' said Aurora, 'and Socrates climbed out of his push-chair. The horse was going very quickly. And then he went off.'

'Oh,' said Father. He stood there for a moment, and then the voice came from the loud-speaker again. 'There's a little boy who has lost his mother. We have him in the office. Please come as quickly as you can.'

'Where is the office?' Father asked the shop assistant. She had picked up the dress and was shaking it out.

'The office is on the third floor,' she said. 'Did you like this one?'

'No thank you,' said Father, 'I don't think it will do.'

He rushed away and went up to the office door and knocked. He was so out of breath that he could scarcely speak. 'Have you got the child here?' he asked.

'Wait a moment,' said a voice. 'What was the child wearing?'

Father looked as if he didn't understand what the lady was saying. 'What was he wearing? Nappies and leggings,' he said, and made to go farther in.

'Yes, all babies wear those,' said the lady firmly. 'What else had he on?'

Father's brain seemed to stop working. He simply couldn't remember whether he had dressed Socrates in his yellow coat or his blue one today, but Aurora knew. 'The yellow one,' she said. 'He had a yellow coat and blue leggings.'

Another lady came into the office. 'Has the mother come to fetch her little boy?' she asked.

'I'm the mother,' said Father. 'I mean, I'm the father, of course.'

'How can we be sure of that?' said the first lady. 'You didn't even know what he was wearing.'

'That's because Daddy has so much to think

about,' said Aurora. 'It's not so easy to take a doctor's degree about the Ancient Greeks, I can tell you, and he's got Socrates and me as well, and has to cook and everything, and today he got the electric light bill, too.'

'That's enough, Aurora,' said Father. 'I'm sure they know that Socrates is our little boy.'

'We'll see what happens when he catches sight of you,' said the lady.

They went into another office, and there was Socrates walking about with the handkerchief in his hand. When he saw Aurora and Father he went more quickly and tried to run away from them, but then it occurred to him that it was a long time since he had seen them and there were a great many strange faces around him.

'Dada,' he said. He held up the handkerchief and flung himself into his father's arms.

'I wonder where you got that handkerchief?' said Father. Socrates clutched it tightly, for this was something he was determined to keep.

'He must have brought it with him from the ground floor,' said the lady.

'Well, we must go down and settle up for it,' said Father. 'Thank you very much for your help. It was kind of you to look after him for us.'

'That's all right,' said the lady. 'He was a good little chap. You must excuse me for asking you some questions before we handed him over, but it might have been someone who heard the announcement and just came and said he was their child.'

'Yes,' said Father, 'you were quite right to make careful inquiries. It was a good thing I had you with me, Aurora.'

'Must you go and look at those dresses again?' asked Aurora.

'No,' said Father. 'We'll go down to the ground floor.' He picked up Socrates and they went down the stairs, and on the way Aurora explained everything about Socrates and about the horse. At the handkerchief counter Father asked how much Socrates' handkerchief cost. 'It's the first time he has bought anything himself,' said Father, 'but I'm sure he hadn't any money on him today.'

It cost two kroner and fifty øre, so Father broke into Granny's hundred kroner note and said, 'Well, that's that. Go and get up on the horse, Aurora.'

'Can I really?' said Aurora.

She went over to the white horse. Luckily there was no one sitting on it now. 'Hold tight, Aurora!' said Father. Then he put in fifty øre, and she began to shake a bit and jump a bit and gallop a bit, and Father stood watching her and smiling.

Socrates sat in his arms and jumped up and

down, even though no one had put fifty øre into Daddy.

When Aurora had finished, she got down from the horse and patted him gently to thank him for the ride. Then Socrates was put in his push-chair and Father wheeled him out of the store.

They went into a little shop, and there Father found a yellow dress and a pretty blouse for Granny, and red boiler-suits for Socrates and Aurora, and there was enough money left to buy a little cap for Socrates and a drink for all three of them.

When they got home, Father had to start getting the dinner. Socrates walked round him holding his fine handkerchief, and Aurora knelt in front of the window and thought about the horse down there in the store.

When Mother came home from the office she said, 'Well, Edward, did you get a lot of work done today?' She looked at him just as if she was sure that he had written the whole of his thesis that morning.

'Work, yes,' said Father, flinging out his arms. 'I did a lot of writing in the tram going into town. I had both the children with me, and we went to the sales, and I was able to study extra hard there, and then – and then . . .'

'Have you all been into town?' asked Mother in surprise.

'Yes, we have,' said Father. 'We went into town for Granny because she wanted a new dress, and she sent money for me to buy something for the children.'

Aurora sat looking from one to the other. She saw that Mummy was upset because Daddy hadn't been able to work, and that Daddy was tired, and sorry that he had spoken as he did.

'I'll sit up late tonight and catch up with my work,' he said. 'At any rate nobody will want food then and there won't be nappies to wash or anything of that sort.'

'As soon as we have eaten, I'll take the children out for a walk,' said Mother, 'and Aurora and I will do the washing-up afterwards, and you can lie down and have a rest, Edward.'

When they were strolling about on Tiriltoppen later on, Mother said, 'Aurora, we must find a way of giving Daddy a chance to work in the days that are left. I wonder what we can do with Socrates?'

'I know,' said Aurora, 'I know someone we could talk to about it.'

A little later they stood outside a door on the thirteenth floor of Block Z and rang the bell.

It was Nusse's mother who opened it.

'Mummy wonders if you could look after Socrates sometimes,' said Aurora.

'Yes, I thought I'd just ask,' said Mother.

'You see, my husband sits up late working every single night, and he would like to work in the morning too, but it's not so easy now that Socrates is big enough to walk about.'

'That's why he looks so worn out, then,' said Nusse's mother. 'It will be quite all right for Socrates to come to me. Nusse is away, and I like company. Will Aurora come too?'

'No,' said Mother. 'Aurora thinks that Socrates would settle down better if he were alone.'

'That's so,' said Nusse's mother, 'he's so fond of Aurora, and it would be better not to have anyone else there talking to him. So you'd better come another time, Aurora. You can come whenever you like, you know.'

'Yes,' said Aurora, 'because we're friends.'

So they went downstairs again, and it was fine that Nusse's mother was going to look after Socrates. But where was Aurora to go?

Aurora thought she was big enough to manage not to disturb Daddy. She could go out all day, and take a lunch-packet with her and sit on a tree stump in the wood, perhaps. As long as Little Bull didn't come that way.

But then Mother said, 'Do you know what you're going to do tomorrow, Aurora dear?'

'No,' said Aurora.

'You'll take a lunch-packet with you,' said Mother.

'Yes,' said Aurora, 'and sit all by myself in the wood and eat it. Can I have some lemonade too?'

'Oh, Aurora!' said Mother. 'You're coming with me to the office, and staying with me until it's time to go home again.'

'I shall be a business-woman, then,' said Aurora with great satisfaction.

8. 'This is Mr Snuvers' Office – Can I Help You?'

THE next morning Father looked like a ghost. Obviously he had been sitting up all night again.

'You shall get some rest today at any rate,' said Mother. 'Socrates is going up to Nusse's mother and Aurora is coming with me.'

'That's fine,' said Father. He yawned, and tried to look wide awake but he didn't succeed.

There was a ring at the door, and there stood Nusse's mother who was up already and quite prepared to take charge of Socrates. Socrates looked at her. He must have thought it was very strange that she had fair hair, for both Mother and Aurora were dark.

As soon as he saw her, he wanted to pull her hair. Luckily Nusse's mother hadn't got a sensitive scalp and only laughed when he tugged as hard as he could. She collected some nappies and other clothes and a few toys, and went off with him, and Socrates gazed at her hair and didn't mind leaving the others at all.

Mother and Father and Aurora sat down again and ate their breakfast. But today a quite new Aurora was there. She had brought an old newspaper to the table, and had poured her milk into a coffee cup. Now she sat there, putting a piece of bread into her mouth from time to time and keeping her eyes fixed on the newspaper. Of course she couldn't read it properly, but she had a good look at all the pictures and thought about what she saw. Now and again she stretched out a hand and picked up the coffee cup. It was a little awkward, because the newspaper was very big and it wasn't easy to hold it in one hand, but she

managed somehow. Then she took a little sip and put the cup down.

'To think that you're going to leave me today!' said Father.

'Mm,' said Aurora. She said no more for some time until she had almost finished eating. Then she quickly folded up the paper and said, 'Have you got my lunch-packet ready, Daddy?'

'Help!' said Mother. 'Is that the way I behave in the morning?'

'Yes, near enough,' said Father, 'but that's all right. Each to his own task – Aurora, your lunch-packet *is* ready.'

'That's good, Daddy,' said Aurora. 'I'll just clean my teeth and then I'll be ready. Do you think I ought to take my umbrella?'

'No,' said Father, 'there isn't a cloud in the sky.' He was joining in Aurora's office game now.

That was a good thing, thought Aurora, because she hadn't got an umbrella.

When she was ready to go, she became Aurora again. She stood and looked at Father who was so pale. 'Are you going to be left here all alone?' she said.

'Yes,' said Father, 'I'm going to work, you see, but it will seem very strange without you, Aurora. I shall miss you very much.'

'I'll come home again, I promise,' said Aurora. 'We'll see each other at dinner-time.'

'Well, well,' said Father. He gave them both a hug, and when Aurora and Mother had got right down to the car, he stood and waved to them with a pink table-cloth so that they should see him.

'Poor Daddy,' said Mother. 'He's worn out, but I don't think there are many days left now before he'll be finished, luckily.'

Mother drove, and Aurora sat behind her and pretended to drive too. They came into the town and went through big streets and small ones. At one point, Mother found a gateway and drove through it into a back yard where several cars were parked. There was just room for Mother's too, but she had to reverse three times before she got into the little space that was left for her.

Then they went out of the gate again and through a door in a building, and up an old staircase which was quite exciting.

It was the kind of staircase that had iron-work patterns between each step. Through the holes in the pattern, Aurora could see straight through the staircase and a long way below. It was a little frightening. It was rather dark here too, and there was a funny smell which Aurora didn't remember although she had been here before. It was an old sort of smell.

When they had climbed three flights of stairs, Mother fumbled in her handbag, found a key, and unlocked a door. They came into Mother's office. It was quite small but it led into a room that was much larger, with a handsome desk and chairs.

'That's Mr Snuvers' room. He's my boss, you know,' said Mother. 'He isn't here today, so it's quite all right for you to be with me.'

Although Mother's office was so small there was room for two people in it.

'We have another man here, you know,' said

Mother, 'a clerk who helps us, but he's on holiday too.'

'Oh,' said Aurora.

'But you can be my clerk today,' said Mother, and cleared away the papers on the other desk. She gave Aurora a sheet of paper and a pencil and a rubber and a stamp. It all looked very business-like, and Aurora had a chair as well that she could swivel round in. She didn't swivel round though, not now, for she realized that she was practically a real business-woman and so she couldn't sit there swivelling round and round.

Mother had taken the cover off the typewriter already, and was typing away at full speed.

From time to time the telephone rang, and Mother picked it up and said, 'Mr Snuvers' office. Can I help you? No, he won't be back for a fortnight. Yes, I'll give him the message. You'll ring later, yes.' Then she rushed back to the typewriter.

A few minutes went by, and the phone rang again and Mother said, 'Mr Snuvers' office. Can I help you? No, he's not here . . .'

'Doesn't anyone ring up and ask for *you*, Mummy?' asked Aurora.

'Oh yes,' said Mother, 'but it doesn't often happen.'

She began to type again, and Aurora understood that she mustn't disturb her.

She sat over in her corner and whispered,
'This is Mr Snuvers' office. She is here. Marie
Tege, yes. She is clever. You ought to ask for
her. She has put off her summer holiday, so
she'll be here for several fortnights yet.'

She said it so softly that Mother didn't hear.
Then Aurora wrote for a little while. She wrote on
an imaginary typewriter, because it was more fun

than writing with the pencil. That didn't look
business-like at all.

There was a little box of paper-clips on her
desk. Aurora pretended it was a telephone, and it
rang at once. She got quite clever at saying 'Mr
Snuvers' office' in the end.

'We'll have our lunch very soon,' said Mother.

'Have we got to be quiet then, too?' asked
Aurora.

'No,' said Mother. 'It's our free time, you see. In the ordinary way I can go out then if I want to, but not now that I'm alone.'

The food tasted very good indeed, and Mother drank coffee from a thermos and Aurora drank lemonade that Father had put in without her knowing it.

'It's so nice to have company, Aurora,' said Mother. 'Do you know what? I'd like to run down and buy us an ice. I'll lock up the office. Do you think you can stay here and look after it? I shall be quicker if I go alone, you see.'

'Of course,' said Aurora.

Mother hurried off, and locked the door on the outside, and Aurora sat there.

Now she was almost like Mother, Mother who had been sitting here by herself every day this summer. Aurora hadn't thought about that before. It was so quiet in here, and so noisy outside. When Mother came back, she would go and sit over there by the window and look out, but she couldn't do that now because she was in charge of the office.

The telephone rang. Not the pretend-telephone, but the real one. Aurora sat and looked at it. It rang and rang and *she was in charge of the office*.

Mother had said so, and she did know what she had to say. The telephone didn't stop. It rang

and rang, and Aurora got up and went over to it.
If it stopped now, she wouldn't need to pick it
up, but if it went on, she would have to. It went
on. Aurora dared not wait any longer before
lifting the receiver. She took the plunge and said,
'Mr Snuvers' office. Can I help you?'

'This *is* Mr Snuvers' was what she thought
she heard, but of course that couldn't be what
the voice had said. It must be *asking* for Mr

Snuvers, for that was what all the others had
done today, and Aurora knew what she had to
say.

'No, he isn't here. He will be on holiday for
another fortnight. You can ring again. Thank
you,' she said, and put the receiver down very
quickly, for the voice in the telephone began to
bellow something or other, 'What's going on?'
or words like that.

Aurora went and sat down in her corner again,

and the next time the phone rang she didn't pick it up, although it seemed to be jumping up and down, it was ringing so loudly. It would just have to go on ringing. At last it stopped, and soon afterwards Mother came back.

'I hope you didn't think I was a long time?' she said. 'I met a colleague in the ice-cream shop and he insisted on telling me where he had been this summer. Hurry up and eat your ice, Aurora.'

Mother had to do the same, for it was beginning to melt.

They ate their ices, and Mother wiped Aurora's mouth, and they both washed their hands, and then Mother sat down at the typewriter again and Aurora stood over by the window. It was so funny to stand up here and look at all the people. It was a wonder they didn't run into each other, they were in such a hurry. Once it almost seemed as if two of them would collide, but then one of them began to step to one side, and the other went in the same direction, and then they gave a little spring from one side to the other and looked as if they were playing a kind of game of their own down there. It was so funny that she couldn't help smiling.

Mother glanced at her and was about to say something. Then they heard a heavy step on the stairs.

'Aurora,' said Mother, 'you can go into Mr Snuvers' office for the time being.'

Aurora nodded, and just as someone knocked on the door, she dashed into the other office and shut the door firmly behind her.

Now she was the boss. She took a good look round. She could walk round and round on the carpet, deep in thought, and then she could peep out of the window, and finally she would go and sit behind the big desk. Nusse's mother ought to have seen it, for it was even shinier than the table in her lounge which was her pride and joy, and it was so big that Aurora could have run her fingers up and down it all day. The chair she sat in had leather arms and it could swivel round as well, quietly, and without a sound.

On the big desk stood a silver-grey telephone with such funny coils in the flex, and there were two buttons to press, a red one and a black one.

Aurora pressed the red one and leant back in the fine office chair again. The door opened and there stood a strange man.

'Who is this?' said the man and bowed.

'I'm the boss,' said Aurora.

'I used to be the boss,' said the man. 'I'm the one who spoke to you on the telephone just now.'

At that point Aurora seemed to wake up. She bolted from the chair and out to Mother, and hid behind her.

But no harm was done, for Mother had explained why Aurora was there, and now the man said, 'Well, well, you must be paid for the time you have been here. Here you are, young lady, here are five kroner, and I've told your mother that you can both have the rest of the day off because I am going to be in town today after all.'

When they were in the car going home, Aurora said, 'Daddy will be pleased.'

'Yes,' said Mother.

'Yes, because he'll have some money to buy dinner with,' said Aurora, and opened her fist which was full of coins.

9. A Happy Day

THE next day Aurora didn't go with Mother to the office. Father said it wasn't necessary. He said he simply didn't work as well if Aurora was away, for he was so used to having her moving quietly about, and she was so good at helping him with everything.

Aurora couldn't help smiling when he said this because it was very nice to hear. But Socrates was too little to help Father, so he went to Nusse's mother that day as well. When he got there he was allowed to empty the kitchen drawer, so he was happy.

Aurora thought about what Father had said, and to make things even better she did everything possible to help him. She washed up after breakfast and made the beds, but when she wanted to take up the rug in the living-room and do the washing in the bathroom, Father said no.

'Wait a bit,' he said, 'can you go and buy us some milk? We must hunt through our pockets first though, because I've spent the five kroner I had from you yesterday. You look in the hall and I'll look in the bedroom.' Aurora went through the pockets of Father's overcoat. There wasn't a single coin, so she looked in Mother's winter coat

and there wasn't anything there either. Aurora began to feel quite depressed. Then she felt in the pockets of Mother's raincoat. There was something there, one, two, three small coins.

Father was rummaging in the pockets of his jacket and he seemed to have found something too. 'How much have you got, Aurora?' he asked. 'Let's see, three ten øre coins, that's fine – I've got a fifty and two fives, and I've two tens here as well.'

They looked at each other delightedly and Aurora ran off to get the milk.

Luckily Mother was paid that day, and when they had fetched Socrates, and eaten porridge with milk and sugar for dinner, they cleared the table and Mother brought in all her money.

They made a number of small piles, one for the rent and one for the electricity bill, and several for food because these were to be for a whole month. It was really frightening that they

were going to eat so much, thought Aurora. There was a pile called 'Sundries' too, and a little one by the side of it which Mother said was called 'Shoes for Aurora'.

Father fetched some envelopes because he thought it would be a good idea to write on them what the money was for.

He sat by the window and wrote 'Rent' on one envelope, and 'Electricity bill' on another, and

'Aurora's shoes' on a third. Mother was going through her bag in case any money was still hidden in it. Aurora stood beside Father, for she felt she must watch him when he wrote 'Aurora's shoes'. So for a moment no one was looking after Socrates. He was toddling round the room but he was not entirely happy because he hadn't found anything to hold in his hand. He made for the table so that he would have something to support him at any rate. It was then that he discovered the pieces of paper that were lying on it. They were exactly what he wanted, but he only needed one of them. Quick as lightning he snatched a hundred kroner note, got a good grip of it, held it up high, and set off round the room at top speed.

Aurora was the first to notice him.

'Oh, look at Socrates!' she said. Mother and Father saw what had happened at the same moment. It was the note for the electricity bill that Socrates had taken.

Aurora wanted to run and get it from him, but Father held her back. 'Don't frighten him,' he said.

'Look, Socrates, here's a spoon for you to hold,' said Mother.

Socrates looked wonderingly at the spoon and took it in his other hand, but dropped it quickly because it just hindered him. The hundred kroner note didn't hinder him, though. It helped him to go from the living-room to the kitchen and back to the living-room again.

Mother took away the other money that was on the table and Father said, 'Put a paper serviette there, will you.'

Then he lifted Socrates up and went over to the window with him. He rocked him gently for a

little while and then he said, 'Mummy goes to town every day and works very hard and earns money so that we can buy food for Socrates. And when Daddy has finished his thesis we're going on holiday, and Mummy has been saving up for it, and Socrates will go with us and drive a long, long way away.'

Socrates laid his cheek against Father and listened wide-eyed, and Aurora thought how sweet he looked. 'So I must take that piece of paper away because we're going to pay for the light with it,' said Father, and held Socrates up to the lamp.

"Ight,' said Socrates.

'Yes, exactly,' said Father, 'and you're going to be a clever boy and help Mummy and Daddy all you can.'

He put Socrates down again, and it looked as if the little boy was thinking about it. Then he fell over, and realized that there was something missing. At first he wondered whether he should get cross, but then he got up and toddled to the table. His tiny fingers reached out to the table top and took hold of something. It was the paper serviette. He seemed to be finding out whether it was a good-for-holding-in-the-hand scrap of paper.

It was all right. He trotted on again, and as the other three were smiling happily at him, Socrates smiled back. He looked extremely pleased with himself as he walked about.

'Socrates understood what you meant, and you didn't scold him,' said Aurora.

'Socrates is a little person who is new to everything,' said Father. 'There's no need to frighten him when we can explain things to him instead.'

Mother nodded, and then Socrates nodded too.

Then Mother and Aurora and Socrates went out for a little walk before bedtime so that Father could get some work done. He worked every night now. He looked very pale at the end of it. But one day when Mother was at the office and Socrates was up with Nusse's mother, Father said, 'Would you like to go into town with me, Aurora?'

'Are we going to the sales?' asked Aurora. She looked so pleased that Father was quite surprised.

'Do you want to go to the sales so much, then?' he asked.

'I was just thinking about that horse,' said Aurora.

'The horse?' said Father. 'Oh yes, that one. We'll see, Aurora. I can certainly do with a new shirt. But that's not the first thing. Guess where I'm going?'

'To the barber's,' said Aurora, for Father hadn't exactly had a recent hair-cut and his face was quite bristly.

'Mm,' said Father, 'that's possible, but this is what I really must do. Look here.' He pointed to a pile of papers. It was his thesis. 'It's finished,' he said.

'Oh!' said Aurora.

'Now we're going into town with it,' said Father.

Aurora was sure they would take the tram, but no, not today. Father went straight over to the taxi rank and said to a driver who was standing there, 'Do you think you could drive us into town?'

'Yes, certainly,' said the taxi-driver. 'Get in, please!'

Father and Aurora sat in the back seat, and Father clutched his briefcase. He was terribly afraid of leaving it behind, and afraid, too, that the taximan might not be a good driver, and supposing they ran into something on the very day when he had this with him! But all was well, and the driver took them right up to the University. Here they got out, and Father said, 'Can you wait out here in the forecourt for a few moments, Aurora, while I go and hand this in?'

Aurora stood there. Crowds of people were walking about in the forecourt, and many were sitting on the steps outside the big building in the middle.

It was here that Mummy and Daddy had got to know each other. It was when they were students, Mummy had told her so.

Perhaps Aurora would come here too when she was grown up. It wasn't certain, of course, for maybe she would sooner be like Nusse's mother and make lots and lots of jam, or perhaps she would be a shop assistant – in that shop where the horse was. Then she would go there early in the morning before all the people came, and sit on it and ride . . .

Father came out again. He looked quite lost, just because he had handed in the work that had cost him so much effort.

'I've done it now, Aurora,' he said, 'and we must hope it will be all right. It's so strange not to have it any longer. I wonder whether I ought to have done it differently . . .'

'Aren't you pleased?' asked Aurora.

'Of course,' said Father, 'I just feel a little empty and strange.'

'Are you going to the barber's?' said Aurora.

'Yes,' said Father and smiled at her.

They went into the barber's shop, and Father sat in a chair and got a white beard of lather that made him look like Father Christmas, but when the barber took a razor and began to shave him, Aurora turned her head away because she found it rather frightening.

Everything was all right, though, and Father looked fine. He gave Aurora a hug, and she turned to the barber and said, 'You were clever, he isn't prickly any more.'

'For as long as it lasts,' said Father, stroking his chin.

'Are you going to buy a shirt now?' asked

Aurora. She was so excited she could hardly breathe.

'Yes, if there's the right sort of shop near here,' said Father.

'Oh no,' said Aurora, 'it must be that special one.'

'Oh of course,' said Father. He went into the big store where they had been before. There stood the horse, waiting for her. Aurora climbed on to its back, and Father put in fifty øre. 'You can have two goes as it's a special day,' he said.

The horse began to shake, and then to jump, and off they trotted.

Father went and bought his shirt.

'Are we going home now?' asked Aurora.

Father shook his head. 'We'll have a little walk,' he said.

They walked until they came to an old brick building that Aurora thought she recognized. They went up a staircase that had ornamental iron-work in between the steps. Aurora knew now where they were. They went up to the third floor, and Father knocked on the door and Mother said, 'Come in. Why it's you two! Are you going to take me home? I'll have finished in two minutes.'

'Fine,' said Father. 'I've finished too.'

'What?' said Mother. 'Have you . . . ?'

'Yes,' said Father, 'and I've handed it in.'

'Oh Edward, congratulations!' said Mother.

'Well, that's a little premature,' said Father. 'We must see how it goes. A lot of people have to read it, you know.'

'It will be all right,' said Mother. 'Oh, I'm so glad! Where is Socrates?'

'With Nusse's mother,' said Father, 'and he can stay there a little longer today.'

'We'll do it, then,' said Mother.

'Do what?' asked Aurora.

'We'll go and have a celebration dinner, the three of us,' said Mother. 'Look here.'

She opened a drawer and took out an envelope. 'For the day Edward finishes his thesis', was written on it.

A little later they were sitting at a table in a restaurant, and a man was playing the piano, and Mother and Father kept squeezing each other's hands because they were so happy. Aurora gave her father's hand a little squeeze too, so that he should know she was there. A waiter came over to them, and Father and Mother discussed a whole lot of different kinds of food, and finally they decided on steak. 'What will you have, Aurora?' asked Father.

'Steak or pancakes?' said Aurora.

The waiter and Father whispered together, and the waiter went away. Soon afterwards he came back with two large steaks and a very small one.

Aurora ate it quite quickly and was still rather hungry. But the waiter came back, and this time he had a dish which was just for her. On it was a large pancake. He put it on a little table which he

had for his own use, and then he set light to the pancake. It flared up and burnt with a blue flame, and it was like this when he brought it to Aurora.

'I'm not angry with you,' said Aurora, 'I know you didn't mean to do it.'

'It was to make it extra-specially nice, Aurora,' Father whispered. 'The pancake is perfectly all right.' And although she had seen the flame with her own eyes, the pancake was whole and tasted absolutely delicious.

When she had finished it, she wasn't hungry any longer.

'Now we must go home to Socrates,' said Mother.

'Oh yes,' said Aurora. Suddenly she thought it was rather a pity that he hadn't been at the celebration too. But probably it wouldn't have been such a good thing, for Socrates would just have walked round to all the other tables and tried to pull off the tablecloths.

'We'll have something extra special at home too,' said Mother, 'and Socrates shall join in.'

Today it was Father who drove them home, and although recently he had hardly had time for anything but reading history and writing, he managed splendidly.

When they reached home, Father and Aurora went straight up to the thirteenth floor to fetch Socrates. Nusse was back from her holiday, and Socrates was waiting for his family to come, because it had been a long day and he hadn't had Nusse's mother to himself any more.

'Now try to say thank you nicely, Socrates,' said Father. 'Thanks to the help they've given us, your Daddy has finished what he had to do.'

'Your Daddy speaks to Socrates in such a

funny way,' whispered Nusse. 'He talks to him exactly as if he were a person.'

'That's what he is,' said Aurora. 'Daddy says that Socrates is a little person who is new to everything.'

'Yes,' said Nusse. 'Look, I can do handstands. I learnt this summer.'

Everybody had to watch Nusse's performance,

and then they went downstairs again. 'See you tomorrow!' Nusse shouted after them.

'Come on, Aurora,' said Father.

'What are we going to have for our celebration at home?' asked Aurora.

'Celebration?' asked Father. He was beginning to feel a little sleepy, for he had sat up last night too.

'Yes, the celebration that Socrates is going to join in,' said Aurora, 'because he wasn't with us in town.'

'Oh yes,' said Father. 'It's a little difficult, because I didn't go shopping today so I haven't bought anything special. But there's some coffee.'

'Socrates doesn't drink coffee,' said Aurora seriously.

'No,' said Father, 'but there's some milk too.'

'That won't make it a celebration,' said Aurora.

'I'm making waffles,' said a voice from the kitchen, 'that will help a bit, won't it?'

'Yes,' said Aurora, 'that will help. Oh, I know, Daddy.'

She went up to him and whispered something. Father nodded, and put his head round the kitchen door. 'Can Socrates come in here with you for a few minutes? Aurora and I are just going on a little errand.'

'Of course,' said Mother, 'off you go.'

Aurora and Father took the lift down to the basement. They went down the long, cold passage. It was very quiet there.

Father unlocked the store-cupboard, and there stood the one jar of jam that he and Aurora had managed to make – the jar that had such a fine label. 'Bilberry and raspberry' was written on it. Father carried it up carefully, and as Mother came in with the waffles, he came in with the jam. Socrates had a little on his plate, and Father gave him a teaspoon so that he could taste it. Socrates tasted it, and then he smacked his lips and licked them. His eyes shone, just as they had done when he had eaten that one bilberry.

Aurora was very happy, for now there was no doubt that Socrates, too, had joined in Father's celebration.

10. A Summer Holiday in November

DURING the next few days Aurora watched Father anxiously. He was doing practically nothing. He had handed in his thesis now, so she had thought that he would have heaps of time to spare, and be very happy. But he just sat in a chair, and didn't make the beds once. It was all he could do to cook the dinner so that Mother had something to eat when she came home from the office.

Mother said it was reaction, and Aurora wondered whether this was an illness, but Mother explained that Father was like this because he had had far too much to do and had used up all his energy so he hadn't any left now. But this would pass, because now at last they were going to have that summer holiday they had put off so long.

Mother rang up a whole lot of different places from the office, but it wasn't as easy as she had thought because many of them had closed now. People didn't take holidays at this time of year, they said. But at last she found a little guest-house in the country which sounded very nice. They had some permanent residents, but they could take Mother and Father and Aurora and

Socrates if they could manage with one room. Mother asked if they could put two cots in it, and they said they would.

She was really pleased on the day when she was able to come home and tell them that everything had been settled. 'The guest-house is called "Plum Tree House",' she said. 'I'm sure we shall be all right there. I'll stay in bed late every morning.'

'Perhaps we shall have breakfast in bed,' said Father.

'I must pack my suitcase,' said Aurora. She had packed it many times already. She had begun in the summer, and put summer clothes in, but she realized she would be too cold in these now, so she put jerseys and a thick skirt and woollen stockings in instead. She went up to see Nusse's mother and told her that she was going on a summer holiday.

'You're going on a summer holiday in November?' asked Nusse's mother. 'You're going to Spain, I suppose.'

'No, I'm going to Norway,' said Aurora.

'You mustn't forget us, then.'

'Of course I won't,' said Aurora.

She told Knut too, but Knut looked glum for he didn't like them going away at all. But when Father asked him if he would water the plants while they were away he cheered up, because he was pleased that Father had chosen him for the job.

Father had come to life again. He was busy packing the big suitcase he was to share with Mother. It was almost full now, and Aurora saw that he was standing looking at a big fat history book. It was as if he were wondering whether the case would protest if he put it in. Finally he stuffed it in between some clothes so that it hardly showed, but all the same Mother found it. 'Do you really need to have that great book with you now, Edward? Can't you give yourself a real holiday?' she said.

'Of course, but it's a good idea to take something I can read aloud to Aurora in the evenings,' said Father, 'and if the weather's bad it will be nice to have an interesting book to pass the time.'

Mother looked as if there were plenty of things she would like to say, but she didn't say them and Father seemed quite relieved.

'I thought of taking some wool and a crochet hook,' said Mother. 'Now that I've plenty of time I should enjoy trying to do some handwork.'

'Can you crochet?' asked Father surprised.

'Yes, I think so,' said Mother, and crocheted a little strip to show what she could do.

'What's it going to be?' asked Father.

'A shawl,' said Mother.

Aurora was so happy that she had to go into

her room and pack her case all over again. Now she looked thoughtfully at the doll that was called Lille-Rora.

'Yes of course you'll come too,' she said, 'although I've very little room in the case, you know.' But when she had put the doll in, the thought came to her that it wasn't very good for her to lie there under the lid. It would be better for Lille-Rora to sit in the car beside her. She was going to take the lovely big poodle that Granny had made for her too; the dog that looked almost real and was called Little Puff.

Socrates was rather scared of Little Puff, but he wasn't scared of Lille-Rora. Aurora often had to put her on the top shelf of the cupboard so that Socrates wouldn't go off with her.

'Just think, Aurora,' said Father. Suddenly he was standing there in the doorway. 'We shan't have to do any washing-up in the guest-house.'

'We'll take Socrates' push-chair so that we can go for long walks,' said Mother.

The only one who didn't say that he was looking forward to the holiday was Socrates. He had only been eight weeks old when they moved to Block Z. He liked the flat, because he was familiar with all the furniture and with all the sounds above and beneath and on either side of them. It was lovely to wake a little while before the others in the morning and lie there practising all the words he knew, and when he had done that for a time, he would stand up and hold on to the high rail round his cot and call to them as loudly as he could so that they should all see what a big fine boy he was. Yes, Socrates enjoyed himself at home, and if they had asked him they would have found out what he felt about go-

ing away. But no one asked him, because they didn't believe he had thought about it.

But Socrates had already begun to notice what was going on. To begin with they had dragged in those things they called suitcases. Now on the whole he had grown accustomed to Aurora's little case because she had packed it so many times, but he had never seen the big case that belonged to Mother and Father, nor the one his own things were to go in. He wouldn't say anything at first, for he was not unreasonable, but on the morning they were to leave, things went too far. Nothing was as it ought to be, and Socrates was in a very bad mood indeed. Father was running round looking for a rope to fasten the cases with, and Mother came to dress him. But she wanted to get it done quickly, and Socrates, who to begin with had just stood there whimpering to himself, got so angry that he wriggled like an eel and wouldn't let her put on a single garment.

'*You* must try, Edward,' said Mother. But although Father said 'bsbsbsbsbs', Socrates was still furious. Mother looked rather relieved at this, because she would have felt hurt if Socrates had only been angry with her.

At last Father put him back into bed again and said, 'Well, Socrates, I'll dress you when you want me to, but you must pull yourself together first.'

For a few moments Socrates was as quiet as a mouse, but then he began to scream as though his life was in danger.

'Oh dear!' said Mother.

'Hm,' said Father. 'What do you think we had better do now? If I go in to him, he will realize that he can do exactly as he likes provided he yells loud enough.'

'Yes,' said Mother, 'and if I go in, he'll think that I didn't agree with what you did.'

'I can go,' said Aurora. She went in to Socrates, lifted him up, and sat down quietly with him on the edge of the bed and let him have a real good cry. He stopped as suddenly as he had started, for he caught sight of his leggings and noticed that a toe was sticking out through a little hole in them. It was his big toe, but it wasn't so very big all the same, and it was bright pink. Socrates looked at it and smiled benignly, and when Aurora took hold of it and said good morning to it very politely, he laughed until he choked.

They all seemed to be running round in circles that morning before they were ready to lock the front door behind them and go along to the lift.

Outside, the little blue car with the red mud-guards was standing waiting for them. It had a luggage-rack on the roof today and looked sturdy enough, but when three cases and a push-chair had been put on the roof, it seemed as though it might find the load too much for it.

'Who's going to drive?' asked Father.

'It looks a bit slippery,' said Mother, 'so perhaps I'd better start.'

'I'm sorry you don't trust me,' said Father. 'It doesn't look as though I shall drive at all, then.'

'Of course you will,' said Mother, 'we'll each do a bit. I only thought you weren't used to slippery roads, but do drive now if you like.'

'No,' said Father, 'I'm not going to.'

Aurora looked from one to the other. 'You sound just like Nusse and Brit-Karen when they're quarrelling,' she said.

Mother and Father looked at each other and Mother said, 'I'm sorry.'

'I'm sorry too,' said Father. 'We mustn't begin our holiday like this. You drive, Marie!'

'No, you drive,' said Mother. It was clear they would never agree.

'Draw lots!' said Aurora.

Father broke a match in two. 'The one who

gets the long end drives first,' he said. Mother drew the short end, so there was no more argument.

To begin with, Socrates sat still and said, 'Toot, toot!' because for a little while he thought it was fun to ride in a car. Now and again he looked out of the window, but after a time he felt he had been quiet long enough. It couldn't be good for him to sit like that all day. He had to exercise his legs and his muscles and explore the world, and the world inside this car was much too small. He tried pulling Aurora's nose a few times, but he got tired of that because he had done it so often before.

When they had been driving for some while Father said, 'It's your turn now, Marie!'

'Socrates is so restless,' said Aurora.

'Is he?' said Father. 'I'd better come and sit in the back with you.'

Aurora had nothing against this. Everything was such fun when Father was sitting with them. There was much more to see as they went along just because they were looking at it together; the black fields with deep furrows in them, and the trees that had no leaves any longer but were so beautiful just then because all their twigs and branches could be seen. Socrates, too, was much quieter now because he had got another nose to pull. Later on, Aurora thought what a good thing it was that Socrates had been restless a little while back.

It all began when they heard some strange noises from Mother.

'Help!' she cried. 'Edward, what shall I do?'

'What is it?' asked Father.

'The brakes won't hold,' said Mother.

They were going down hill, and suddenly the car seemed to want to cross the road instead of keeping straight ahead, and although Mother braked as hard as she could, it wouldn't stop – it just kept on sliding. The reason was that there was a thin sheet of ice on the surface of the road, and perhaps Mother had been going too fast before she realized that she was driving on a kind of skating-rink. Now as they slid along, Mother said, 'What shall I do?'

'Just sit still and try not to run into anything,' said Father.

It was to be hoped they wouldn't meet another car at this particular moment! They didn't do that, but they *did* meet a tree. It wasn't in the road, but it was growing by the side of it, and the car seemed to be attracted by it. Aurora was glad then that Socrates had been restless, for the car met the tree on the side where Father would have been sitting, and there was the tinkle of glass as the window shattered.

At least the car had come to a stop now.

Father got out and looked at it. He gazed up and down the road and saw something that pleased him. It was a heap of sand. Men must have been working on the road a little lower down and they had left a big heap of sand behind them. He took a spade and threw sand over the road in front of the car. Then he looked at Mother. She was terribly upset.

'It was a good thing you didn't run into a car,' said Father. 'We might have made a dent in the other car too and had to pay a lot of money. But the tree won't ask for compensation.'

'Have I understood you correctly?' he said, and bowed to the tree, and then Mother had to laugh, and so did Aurora. Socrates looked and looked at the tree, and didn't think it in the least funny that Father should bow to it.

'You must drive now,' said Mother. 'Now that I've been so stupid I don't think I dare go on.'

'Yes, you must,' said Father. 'That's just what you must do.' He sat in the back seat again.

The wheels of the car decided to turn, and Mother drove very carefully, and although it was rather cold because of the broken window, they got along all right and didn't stop until they came to a little place where there was a service station and petrol pumps.

There they got help with the window so that they shouldn't freeze during the journey, but they left the big dent alone. They hadn't the time or the money to do anything about that.

When they drove on, Father took Socrates on his lap and hummed and sang funny little tunes into his ear, and soon Socrates fell asleep. Aurora realized that she was tired too. It would have been nice now to be as little as Socrates. Then she could have sat on Father's lap and been rocked to sleep. However, she laid her head on his shoulder, and soon she was asleep too.

The days were very short now, and when Aurora woke up, Mother had put the car lights on. The trees were so dark and still that it was exciting just to sit inside the car and look at them.

'You must help me now to look for the signposts,' said Mother. 'It can't be very far away.'

'There's something over there,' said Father. 'Summer road to Plum Tree House' said the notice. They stopped, and Mother and Father got out of the car. The summer road was very steep, and when they looked at it more closely they saw that it was icy too. 'I think we'll leave the car down here on the road,' said Father, 'and then we can fetch it early in the morning.' He didn't want to run into any more trees that day.

Father unfolded the push-chair so that Socrates could sit in it, and strangely enough Socrates didn't protest, because it was dark outside and rather cold, and everything was so different from what he was used to. He ought to have been in the living-room at home now, having his supper.

'Do you think you can manage Socrates, Aurora?' asked Father.

'Yes, of course,' said Aurora. She began to

wheel her brother up the steep, narrow road. But what was happening? She wanted her legs to go up hill, but instead they kept slipping back, and when she slipped, the push-chair slipped as well. This made Socrates laugh, because he thought they were playing the game in which his push-chair rolled down hill by itself.

'I'll help you,' said Mother, 'I've only one case to carry.'

For a little while all was well, but suddenly Mother called out, 'I'm slipping!' She slid back and Socrates went with her. He laughed until he almost cried, and shouted, 'More, more!'

'I think I had better carry the cases up on my own first,' said Father, 'and get hold of some sand that I can throw down for you to walk on, ladies, as you're so helpless as soon as you get out into the country.'

'Well, listen to that!' said Mother. 'I won't answer you now,' she added, but Aurora could hear the laughter in her voice. Father started off with the suitcases. He walked quickly and steadily up the hill. Aurora watched him as long as she could because she didn't like him to leave them.

Then she thought she heard a shout, and something came whizzing down the hill.

'Look out, Aurora!' cried Mother.

It was one of Father's suitcases that seemed to

be out on its own, and after it came another one, and finally Father himself. It looked as though he had sat down and tobogganed down the slope on his overcoat. The big suitcase had hit a stone and the lid had come open. They picked up everything they could see, and shut it again.

'We ought to have brought a torch,' said Father. 'Remember that, the next time we have a summer holiday in November, Marie. We'll put the push-chair in the car and walk over this field. At least it won't be so slippery. I'll take Socrates and the heaviest suitcase. Can you manage the others?'

'Of course,' said Mother. She was laughing

now. They set off in the dark with the cases over the rough ground.

They saw the house a long way above them. Its lighted windows looked so friendly that they knew they were on the right road, or rather on the right field. It took them a long time to reach it. 'Why, there's a car outside the house!' said Mother. 'It must have been there since last summer.'

'I'm sure there's another road up,' said Father. 'We ought to have driven on a bit.'

A lady was standing at the top of the steps. 'I thought I heard voices,' she said, 'but where's your car? Didn't you say on the phone that you were coming by car? Surely you haven't come by train and walked from the station?'

'Oh no,' said Mother, 'we just thought the road was very steep so we left the car down below.'

'Oh, that's our summer road,' said the lady. 'We use the other one in winter. Do come in.' Inside the hall it was so warm that it almost took Aurora's breath away, for a stove was roaring and burning so fiercely that there was a glow all round it.

'I expect you would like to go up to your room first,' said the lady, starting to climb the stairs. 'It's a little cramped up there as you wanted us to put in two cots. We didn't use the room in the autumn, but there's been a fire in there all day so it ought to be warm now. Oh, what a dear little boy!' she said, looking at Socrates. 'I'm glad he seems so quiet! I feel I must tell you that I have a number of elderly guests, and you know they don't like to be disturbed in the morning or during their afternoon rest.'

'Oh yes,' said Father, and looked thoughtfully at Socrates.

Their bedroom was pink with bright blue window sills and red checked curtains.

'There's water in the jug on the washstand,' said the lady, 'and we shall be eating in a quarter of an hour. I expect you would like to put the little boy to bed first.'

'That won't be any good,' said Mother, 'because he's slept for hours during the journey.'

'All right then,' said the lady. 'We ring a bell when the meal is ready.'

They had to change Socrates first for he was soaking wet. It wasn't his fault, of course, because he had been sitting in the car all day.

Soon afterwards all four of them were ready and went downstairs. Father had Socrates in his arms. They passed the fiercely-burning stove. 'Phew!' said Father, 'that's hot!' 'Ooh!' said Socrates.

They went into a room with a lot of red plush chairs. Three elderly ladies and a gentleman with a white beard were sitting there. There was a great deal of handshaking, and Aurora thought she would never stop having to curtsey, but it was over at last and they were summoned to the dining-room.

'We haven't got a high-chair for Socrates,' whispered Aurora.

'I'll take him on my lap,' said Father.

First a maid in a black dress and white apron came in with several plates of hot soup. This wasn't exactly suitable for Socrates, but Father tried to eat his own soup as quickly as he could. It wasn't easy, for Socrates made a grab at his spoon every time he lifted it from the plate. Once he managed to get hold of it, and jerked the spoon so that the soup splashed the face of the lady who was sitting next to Father.

'Oh, I'm so sorry!' said Father. Mother got up and wiped the lady with her table-napkin.

'He's not used to being away from home,' said Mother.

One of the other ladies laughed. 'O-oh! He reminds me of my own little boy,' she said.

'Have you got a little boy too?' asked Aurora happily. 'Has he gone to bed?'

The lady laughed even more. 'He's over fifty,' she said, 'but he was just like that when he was little.'

The lady who had been splashed with soup tried to smile too. 'Yes, they are sweet at that age,' she said, 'but perhaps the dinner-table isn't the best place for them.'

The waitress came in again with a large dish of smoked ham and mutton.

It wouldn't have been very good for Socrates to eat that either. Aurora looked at Mother, and Mother whispered something to the waitress. By now Socrates was frantic with hunger, but at last a big slice of bread with a piece of cheese on it and a cup of milk arrived for him. Socrates fell upon the bread and picked off the cheese in a tremendous hurry. Then he began to eat and everyone sighed with relief, but he must have eaten much too fast because he choked. He coughed and spluttered, and bread flew in all directions.

Then Mother got up. 'I'll take him upstairs,' she said. 'I've had something to eat. Now you can have your meal in peace, Edward.' She took the slice of bread and Socrates with her.

'Now you really must eat something,' said the lady who had been splashed with soup. 'Poor man, you haven't had a single bite.'

'Yes I have, *one*,' said Father smiling.

11. At the Guest-House

WHEN Aurora woke the next morning, Socrates and Father had both disappeared, but Mother was lying in bed and was still asleep, which was just what she had looked forward to while she was on holiday. Aurora didn't wake her but began to dress as quietly as she could. The worst of it was that it was so cold in the bedroom. Aurora had a good idea. As it was so cold, she would dress under the bedclothes where it was nice and warm, and when she sat there she was in a little room of her own. But she was slower like this.

While Aurora was keeping as quiet as she could, she heard someone walk down the passage, and then a girl came into the room. No doubt she had knocked on the door as best she could, but it wouldn't have been easy, for she was carrying a great armful of wood. She went straight to the stove and began to lay the fire.

Aurora forgot about dressing for the time being, for this was fun to watch. Newspapers and wood-shavings and sticks were put in the stove. At first there was only a tiny flame, but then it grew, and more and more flames sprang up and began to lick the wood until the fire was burning properly. The girl who had laid it smiled at Aurora and waited a minute or two. Then she looked inside the stove and turned a little wheel in the door so as to leave a small opening. Then she nodded, and slipped out of the room. She hadn't looked at Mother at all, and Mother hadn't noticed anything. She must have been very tired. Aurora finished dressing quickly and went out of the door.

It was exciting to come out into the corridor, for yesterday she hadn't been able to look round properly. She peeped out of the window, but there wasn't a great deal to see because it was still dark. She could just glimpse an outhouse and some dark mountain ridges and some trees. Suddenly Aurora was terribly glad to be on holiday, but when she came into the big sitting-room she felt a little uneasy. There was nobody there, and the red plush chairs seemed to be looking at her just like the lady who had been splashed with soup. Aurora went on to the dining-room. Where were Daddy and Socrates, then? Surely they hadn't gone out so early? It was much too cold for Socrates.

There wasn't anyone in the dining-room either, but there would certainly be breakfast there because the table was laid with egg-cups and plates and jam and a goat-cheese that was so big that it would last for a year at least. The sight of that table made Aurora hungry, but she wouldn't eat until she found Daddy.

Then she heard voices. They seemed to come from the kitchen. Should she go in, she wondered. It sounded as though they were laughing and talking and having such a good time. Aurora peeped round the door. Oh, how cosy and bright and warm it was, and who was that sitting beside Daddy on a wooden bench behind the long table? Yes, it was Socrates. He was happy and contented and was eating bread and drinking milk.

'Hallo, Aurora,' said Father. 'Here we are.'

A young woman in a white apron was standing there. 'So you're Socrates' sister, are you?' she said.

'Yes,' said Aurora. She looked at Socrates. It must be such fun to sit and eat at that table.

'Socrates and I have been up for some hours already,' said Father. 'He was making such a racket that I just had to take him downstairs so that the ladies in the next room shouldn't be disturbed. We were glad to find our way to the kitchen, I can tell you.'

'Perhaps the little girl is hungry too,' said the young woman in the white apron.

'Yes, I am,' said Aurora. She didn't take long to reach the table. Although Socrates had his mouth full of bread, he patted her arm as if to show that he was glad to see her.

Aurora was given a large slice of bread with goat-cheese, and some milk. How good that bread tasted!

'Can't we be here all the time when we're indoors?' asked Aurora.

'You can come here as often as you like,' answered the young woman in the white apron.

'She's called Olaug,' said Father, 'and she's

given me eggs and bacon and coffee. She's awfully nice.'

'Ah, but I'm not afraid to speak my mind,' said Olaug.

'That's good,' said Father, 'because then I can rely on you to tell me if it's not convenient for us to be in here.'

'Just you come,' said Olaug. 'It's not easy for a little one to sit at table as long as the grown-ups want to.'

Aurora was watching Socrates. He ate and ate,

but his eyes began to look funny. They seemed
to roll round, and now and then his eyelids
closed. Then he woke up and went on chewing
for a moment, but soon his eyelids closed again.

'Daddy,' said Aurora, 'Socrates is tired.'

'So am I,' yawned Father. 'Socrates and I can
go and sleep now and you must keep Mummy
company when she comes down.'

'All right,' said Aurora. 'Can I stay here until
she comes?'

'Certainly,' said Father.

Aurora sat there on the long wooden bench,
and the three other people in the kitchen joked
and laughed. Two of them teased Olaug about
her sweetheart, and then they all laughed so
loudly that Aurora couldn't help laughing too
although she didn't know whom they were talking about. It was lovely to be there. They didn't
ask her any questions, and she didn't feel the

least bit lonely. Once Olaug came over to her with a biscuit with cheese on it, and one with jam. But after a little while she heard voices from the dining-room, and when she looked in, Mother was there with the strangers. Aurora hurried in and sat down beside her.

'Good morning, Aurora dear,' said Mother. 'Have you had breakfast already?'

'Your husband is still asleep, I expect,' said the lady who had been splashed with soup yesterday. 'Men seem to need more sleep than we do, and now that he's on holiday I think you're right to let him have a good lie in.'

'We neither of us slept much last night,' said Mother, 'because our little boy isn't used to being away from home. He didn't like being in a strange bed, so we took it in turns to nurse him most of the night.'

'Oh, it's just as though I were hearing about my own little boy,' said the other lady. 'He was always so restless when he was in a strange place.'

'Yes, it's very easy to spoil them,' said the soup lady, whatever she might have meant by that.

When they had finished breakfast, Mother whispered, 'Aurora, will you come with me and fetch the car while Daddy and Socrates are asleep?'

'Yes,' said Aurora. They went upstairs and got their outdoor clothes and slipped out of the room again.

'I'm so glad we didn't wake them,' said Mother.

When they got outside, Aurora realized that the air here was quite different from the Tiril-toppen air. It was so cold that it made her nose tingle, but she liked the feeling. It was lovely to be going out with Mother to explore everything.

They didn't take the summer road this time. They went on the road they should have taken, which made a series of long bends and gave them a view of the whole valley.

At last they caught sight of the car. It stood there all alone, waiting for them. It had had a really hard knock when it hit that tree yesterday, and Aurora thought it looked rather sorry for itself. But it will be all right now, she said to herself.

While the others were out, Father had slept soundly at first, but now he was beginning to wake up. It wasn't because of Socrates, for he still had a lot of sleep to make up.

Father sat up in bed and wondered what he should do. Why, of course, he could read that book he had brought with him. He felt very pleased to have thought of it, and he went over to the big suitcase he shared with Mother. Well, that was funny! This was where he had put it. Perhaps Mother had unpacked it.

He looked on the table, and on the chest of drawers and in all the drawers, but there was no book to be seen. The only thing he found was Mother's crochet-work which was on top of the

case. Had Mother really played a trick on him and taken the book out because she wanted him to have a real holiday and not read any history?

Father looked hard at the crochet-work. Since she had been mean enough to remove his book, he would get his own back. He took out Mother's crochet-work and hid it between the back of the chest of drawers and the wall. It wouldn't be easy to find there, at any rate. When he had done this, he dressed, and when the others drove up to the house he stood at the window and watched them. Mother and Aurora waved, and Father waved back, and put his finger to his lips to show that Socrates was still asleep.

But when Mother came in, she spoke in her ordinary voice so that Socrates should wake up, because she thought that if he slept all day he would be awake at night again.

'Thank you, Daddy, for being our baby-sitter,' said Mother.

'I'll be glad to baby-sit as often as you like,' said Father, 'but I'd like to have something to read while I'm doing it. It's a pity I haven't anything.'

'Haven't you got that fat history book of yours, then?' asked Aurora.

'I thought I had,' said Father, looking hard at Mother.

'Well,' said Mother, 'I feel rather cold now and I'm glad to be indoors again. I think I'll take my crochet-work and go downstairs and talk to the other guests. They're really very nice when you get to know them, especially the lady who is always talking about her own little boy.'

'I'll put Socrates in his push-chair and go for a

walk,' said Father. 'Will you come too, Aurora?'

'Yes,' said Aurora, for although she had walked such a long way already, she wanted to go out again because it was such fun, and Daddy would be with her and she could show him everything she had discovered.

'I'll take Little Puff,' she whispered.

Mother was rummaging in the suitcase. 'What on earth have I done with my crochet-work?' she said. 'I put it in here.'

'Yes, just like my book,' said Father, giving her a funny look again.

'I think we must both have gone crazy,' said Mother, laughing.

'Oh no,' said Father, 'we're certainly not crazy.' He picked up Socrates and strode out of the room, and although Mother found his behaviour rather odd, she didn't think much more about it.

When Father got down to the hall, he thought that perhaps Socrates might be hungry again. 'Wait here a moment, Aurora,' he said, 'while I take Socrates into the kitchen and ask for a slice of bread for him.'

'For me too,' said Aurora.

'All right,' said Father, 'but there's no need for all three of us to go through the sitting-room.'

While Aurora was waiting for Father, three of the guests came in. They must have been out for a walk, but my goodness, how agitated they looked!

'I'm pretty sure the proprietress has telephoned the authorities,' said the soup lady.

'Yes, that's the safest thing to do,' said the lady with her own little boy.

'Yes, because the thief may be hiding in the neighbourhood,' said the third.

Then they caught sight of Aurora. 'Is there a thief here?' she asked.

'Don't be afraid. We haven't seen him,' said the soup lady, 'but there's a car outside that looks as if it's a write-off. Somebody must have stolen it in the town because it has an Oslo number, and there's something odd about the paintwork. It's blue, with red mudguards, and the thief must have done that so that no one should recognize it, and then he had a collision – no doubt he was speeding to get away from the police, or something of the sort. What impudence to leave it right outside the guest house!'

'It's – it's ours, it's our car,' said Aurora and held Little Puff in front of her as a protection.

'Oh my goodness, is it?' said the soup lady. 'Oh well,' she said, 'I suppose your father is just like other young men. He drives too fast and then you run into something!'

'Daddy wasn't driving,' said Aurora, 'it was Mummy, and there was ice too.'

'Oh I see,' said the lady with her own little boy. 'Well, I'm glad to hear it, Aurora, for I shall be able to sleep soundly tonight and not have to sit up because I'm scared of thieves.'

They disappeared upstairs, and Father came back with Socrates. 'Now we'll go for a walk, Aurora,' he said.

'What's a write-off?' asked Aurora.

'It's a car that's ready for the scrap-heap,' said Father.

They went outside, and Father looked at the car and at the dent in it and said, 'Hallo, I wonder whether Aurora has been talking about you to anyone? We shan't use you today because we want some fresh air.'

'The car's having a holiday too,' said Aurora.

'It looks as if it needs one,' said Father. 'Come along, Aurora, let's go and discover new country.'

12. Educating Socrates

LITTLE PUFF looked as if he were out for a walk. Aurora kept a firm hold on him, but there was one small difficulty. She had to hold him so that Socrates couldn't catch sight of him, for Socrates was afraid of him. He wasn't afraid of real dogs, just of Little Puff, and that was a pity, for Aurora often had to stop playing with him so that Socrates wouldn't start screaming.

But he didn't scream today, although Aurora was almost certain that he had seen that she had her dog with her.

'Socrates,' said Father, 'you're in the country now, and the houses you see around you are called farms. Do you know what I've thought of, Aurora? Socrates has never seen a pig except in pictures.'

'Mm,' said Aurora, 'he's seen a cow, though.'

'Only just,' said Father. 'He didn't come into the cowshed with us that time we went to see Rosie.'

'It's a pity it's not summer,' said Aurora, 'then there might have been some out of doors.'

'Yes,' said Father. He looked searchingly at the farms round about.

Every time they passed a big farm, he stopped

and thought about it, but then he sighed and went on, for it wasn't so easy just to go in and say, 'Here's Socrates and he has never seen a pig.'

But when they had walked a long way uphill, they came to a small farm that was perched high up and seemed to look out over the whole valley.

'That looks nice,' said Aurora. 'Perhaps we could go in there?'

'Yes,' said Father.

'There's a little boy sitting on the steps,' said Aurora.

Father leant over the fence and said, 'Hallo! What's your name?'

The boy didn't answer. He just ran into the house as quick as lightning, but when Aurora looked more closely, she saw several small heads at the windows.

A moment later, a woman came out into the yard, and Father said, 'Please excuse us for standing here staring, but we thought what a lovely situation this farm has. You've got a wonderful view.'

'Yes, it's about the only thing we have got,' said the woman, smiling.

'Have you got a pig?' asked Aurora.

'Why yes,' said the woman, looking rather surprised.

'I think I can see some little faces at the

windows,' said Father, 'so maybe there are some children here?'

'Yes, I've got four little ones and a big one.'

The children had come out on the steps now, and Socrates stood up in his push-chair. 'Boy, boy,' he said.

'What are these youngsters called, then?' asked Father. 'I asked one of them but he wouldn't tell me.'

'There's Oddmund and Arne and Benedict and Baby and I've got a big boy called Peter. He's very fond of reading and he's at home today.'

'Doesn't he go to school, then?' asked Father.

'Oh yes, but they go to school every other day here,' said the woman. 'What are your children called?'

'Aurora and Socrates,' said Father.

'*Socrates*,' said the children, staring. 'Socrates!' They rushed into the house and Aurora could hear them shouting, 'Peter, there's a boy here who's called Socrates!'

'Why on earth are they so taken with the name?' asked Father in surprise.

'Well, a funny thing happened yesterday,' said the woman. 'Our eldest lad had been to an evening class at the school and came home late, and as he was walking up the steep path he stumbled against something. When he put his torch on to see what it was, he found a big book, and he read it to us yesterday evening, and it was about a fellow called Socrates. Come in and I'll show it to you.'

They went into a small room. It was clean and bright, with a big wide bed against one wall. A boy sat at the table, reading.

Aurora stared, wide-eyed. It was Daddy's big book lying there on the table. It was the one he had put in the suitcase. Suddenly she remembered what had happened when they were climbing up to the guest-house yesterday evening. Daddy had disappeared into the darkness with two suitcases; then one of them had come whizzing down again and hit against something and burst open. The book must have jumped out, and they hadn't seen it because they hadn't got a torch with them.

She was about to speak her thoughts aloud, but Father pressed her arm and shook his head.

'Do you like reading history?' he asked the boy.

'I'll say I do,' answered the boy.

'He'll have to give the book up, though, because it must belong to someone at the guest-house,' said his mother. 'But I've promised him he can read it first.'

'I'll tell you what,' said Father. 'The book is mine, but let's say, Peter (that's your name,

isn't it?), that I can borrow it while I'm on
holiday and afterwards you can have it back. It
will be your very own and I will write "To
Peter from Edward" in it, so that there's no
doubt it belongs to you.'

Aurora could see that Peter was very pleased,
but all the same he wasn't quite sure that he
would get the book back, for he looked longingly
at it when he handed it over.

'You'll get it all right,' said Aurora, 'because
Daddy always keeps his promises.'

'That's really good of you,' said his mother.

'There's just one thing,' said Father. 'Our Socrates has never seen a pig. Do you think you could show him one now?'

They all looked so astonished that Aurora nearly burst out laughing. But Peter's mother said, 'Of course he can see a pig.'

They went into the pigsty which was next to the cowshed. Socrates kept quite quiet while they were in there. 'Nuff, nuff,' said Father.

When they came out into the yard, Father wanted to go on and have a good walk, but Aurora said, 'I don't want to go for a walk, I want to stay here. May I, Daddy?' Socrates didn't ask, he just climbed out of the push-chair where Father had put him, and began to stump about: there were certainly plenty of nursemaids and playmates here.

'Are you sure they don't mind your staying here?' asked Father.

'Of course we don't mind. It will be a treat for us too,' said Peter's mother.

The children didn't talk much more than Socrates, but all the same it was fun to be with them. Aurora saw their toy cowshed which was built of small stones and had proper stalls inside it, and finally they showed her the real cowshed too. Socrates was a bit scared, because two of the cows *said* something when he came in.

The children were very taken with Little Puff. They thought he was much better than cows and pigs although he was made of black wool.

Luckily Father wasn't away long, and when he came to fetch them, Aurora asked if they might come here every day. She was beginning to enjoy this holiday because she had made friends with some children now, and she could be in the kitchen at the guest-house, and go for walks with Mummy and Daddy and Socrates.

When they got home, an unexpected sight met their eyes. Mother had taken all the mattresses off the beds. They were standing against the wall and the room looked rather dreary. Socrates didn't like it and hid his face in his hands. But Mother said, 'At all events they will be warmed right through and we shan't freeze tonight. Whatever have you got under your arm, Edward?'

'Well, a lot of funny things happen in this world,' said Father, 'and this time I've been unjust to you. I was absolutely sure that you had taken this book out of the suitcase so that I shouldn't do any reading during the holiday. But do you know where I found it?'

'In your overcoat pocket,' said Mother, but as soon as she had said it she knew it was a silly answer because that thick book would never go into the pocket of Father's overcoat.

'No,' said Father. 'Come over to the window and you'll see.'

Mother looked over the valley, but Father said, 'No, you must look up. Do you see that little farm away up there?'

The sun was shining on it and seemed to be showing Mother which one it was.

'That's where I found the book,' said Father, 'and it will go back there.'

Then he told her the whole story, and Aurora sat on his lap and put in a whole lot of details herself so that Mother would be sure to understand it. Socrates said, 'Nuff, nuff,' for Father had told him that that was what the pig said.

When Father had finished his story, he said,

'Well, now I must do my good deed and perform a little conjuring trick – no, on second thoughts we'll play a game. You must try to find something, Mummy.'

'What am I to look for, then?' asked Mother. 'Oh, my crochet-work! Did you take it, Edward?'

'Yes, it was to get my own back,' said Father, 'and I really am sorry.'

'It was a good thing after all that I couldn't find it,' said Mother, 'or I wouldn't have turned all the mattresses over.'

To begin with she looked under the beds. 'You're cold,' said Father.

'Tell me where it is, Daddy,' said Aurora, 'it's such fun to know.'

Father whispered in her ear.

'You're cold!' shouted Aurora when Mother went near the door.

But when at length she went over to the chest of drawers, Aurora and her father both shouted, 'You're getting warm, you're getting warm!'

First of all Mother looked in all the drawers and then they shouted. 'You're getting colder!' But when at last she started to look behind the chest of drawers they yelled, 'You're burning!' at the top of their voices.

'That's it then,' said Mother. 'Oh you wretch! Take that!' She was thumping Father with the ball of wool, when the door opened and the soup lady put her head in. 'I thought you were shouting that something was burning,' she said. 'If there's a fire, do tell me. I have a lot of valuable things with me and I'd like to know if I ought to get them out.'

'Oh no,' said Mother. 'I'm sorry, we didn't realize you were in your room. We were playing a game.'

'Oh I see,' said the lady. She looked at the mattresses on the floor and said, 'I usually have a little rest before dinner.'

'I'll take Socrates downstairs,' said Mother, 'then you won't be disturbed any more.'

'Well, it wasn't exactly his fault,' said the lady, but she nodded and went away.

However, it wasn't very easy to have Socrates in the sitting-room, for there were so many things there that he could break.

When Aurora came down a little later, Mother and Socrates were not there. They were in the kitchen, and Socrates was having an early dinner of fish cakes and grated carrot. When he had finished, he was allowed to clear out the kitchen drawer.

'I wonder if we can get Socrates to sleep before we have our meal today?' said Mother. They took him upstairs: he must have been quite tired, for he had been out to play, and had been taken for a long walk, and had been working in the kitchen as well. He let them wash him and change him, but as soon as they laid him down in his cot, he knelt up again and said, 'Not Socates' bed, not Socates' bed.'

'If only we had thought of bringing his own eiderdown,' said Mother. 'He hasn't got anything here that reminds him of home.'

Then Aurora happened to think of Lille-Rora. Socrates had often reached out for her, for he liked this doll, but Aurora had said, 'No, Socrates, Lille-Rora is mine.' But now she had Little Puff, and perhaps Lille-Rora would be glad to belong to someone who had heaps of time for her. Aurora went over to her bed and fetched her. As soon as Socrates caught sight of her he stopped crying.

'Here you are, Socrates,' said Aurora.

How pleased Socrates was! He clutched Lille-Rora to him, and pulled at her dress, and stroked her face, and pressed his forehead against hers and stared into her eyes. He paid no attention to the other three. He wouldn't lie down, though; there was no question of that, for it wasn't his bed.

He sat there until he fell back, overcome by sleep, and Lille-Rora did the same and slept too, happy that she had somebody to talk to her again.

'That was very nice of you, Aurora,' said Mother. 'Thank you.'

'Can Little Puff come down to dinner, do you think?' asked Aurora.

'Yes, I don't think any of the other guests are afraid of him,' said Father.

When they got downstairs, Aurora was very surprised because everybody seemed so pleased to see them.

'We were afraid you weren't coming down to dinner,' said the soup lady.

'We've just got Socrates off to sleep,' said Mother.

'I saw that your Daddy took you both for a walk today, Aurora,' said the lady who was always talking about her own little boy. 'We're having a joint for dinner.'

Aurora was very pleased, because they hardly ever had a joint at home. It tasted delicious. It tasted delicious until the ladies began to talk to Father.

'What do you do, then, Mr Tege?' asked the soup lady.

'History,' said Father. 'Ancient history.'

'That must be interesting,' said the lady. 'Where do you work?'

At that moment Father had a large piece of potato in his mouth and he could only just manage to answer. 'Tiriltoppen, Cranberry Way, Block Z,' he said at length.

'My husband works at home,' said Mother.

'Yes, it's all right to work at home when you have such a charming wife to look after you,' said the gentleman with the white beard. He meant to pay Mother a compliment, but she laughed and said, 'Poor Edward, he doesn't get much looking after because I go off to the office every day.'

'Daddy's terribly clever,' said Aurora, 'and so is Mummy.'

'I can well believe it,' said the lady. 'Of course you'll have domestic help. Have you managed to get hold of a capable person whom the children like?'

'Yes, indeed,' said Mother. 'I'm a bit jealous sometimes, because I think the children are fonder of the help than they are of me.'

'Oh no,' said Aurora, 'we're just as fond of both of you, but perhaps Socrates is more used to him at meal times.'

'Is your help a man?' asked the lady in surprise.

'Yes,' said Aurora, 'it's Daddy.'

'Oh, you're joking,' said the lady.

'Very likely not,' said the lady with her own little boy. 'My husband often stayed away from business to be at home with our boy, he was so afraid that he would never get to know him properly.'

No sooner had she said this than they heard a queer, wailing noise somewhere in the house. It came nearer and nearer, and then the door opened. A little figure in a white sleeping-suit staggered in. His face was tear-stained, and Lille-Rora hung head down in his arms and almost seemed to be crying too.

'Ma-da,' howled Socrates, for this was what he said when he meant both of them.

'I'll take him, Marie,' said Father. 'It's my turn today and it will be yours tomorrow.'

'This is a funny sort of holiday,' said Mother, shaking her head.

When Mother and Aurora went upstairs after dinner, Father had gone to bed and was reading his big, fat book. Socrates lay in his arms, and Lille-Rora lay on his head, for Socrates thought that was a very good place for her.

'Is it all right if Aurora and I go for a little stroll?' whispered Mother.

'Of course,' said Father, 'but don't get lost.'

'We won't,' said Mother.

13. In the Dark

OUTSIDE the house there was a little lamp that shone brightly, but beyond there was nothing but the dark . . .

'Perhaps we'd better just walk round and round here,' said Aurora, 'because we shan't be able to see anything down on the road.'

'We'll go a little way all the same,' said Mother, 'it's exciting.'

It was queer to go from the light into the darkness. 'I've never seen the dark before,' said Aurora. It was strange and soft and she felt she could almost touch it.

'We'll walk on a bit and you'll find that your eyes get used to it,' said Mother.

'Yes,' said Aurora. She would have liked to

say a lot more, but somehow the words wouldn't come out.

However, it was as Mummy had said. After a little while it became easier to see, not that she could see very much, but at least she knew where the road was, and the road seemed a bit lighter than the rest. Mummy spoke now and then, but quietly. That sounded right to Aurora. She wouldn't have liked it if Mummy had talked loudly now.

'There are lights in some houses,' said Aurora.

'Yes,' said Mother.

'They're quite a long way away,' said Aurora. 'The one up there must be the little farm we told you about.'

'Be quiet a minute,' said Mother. They stood quite still for a moment.

'There's somebody walking along the road,' said Aurora.

'Mm,' said Mother. She didn't say any more but it seemed to Aurora that she began to walk a little faster.

'It's lovely to have an evening stroll, isn't it?' said Mother.

'Yes, it is,' whispered Aurora. Although they were walking quickly, she and Mother put their feet down carefully so that they could scarcely be heard. The other person could be heard quite clearly, he had such a heavy tread, but luckily he wasn't walking fast, thought Aurora.

They saw the lights of the little farm quite distinctly now. They could see small windows that shone and twinkled at them, and round the windows there was something dark and angular that was the house itself.

'Shall we go in when we get there?' said Aurora.

'Yes, that would be nice,' said Mother. She sounded very pleased that Aurora had suggested it. 'Do you think we can?'

'Of course,' said Aurora. 'They said I was to come and see them again.'

Mother began to walk terribly fast, and it was all that Aurora could do to keep up with her. At last they reached the gate. It was a good thing that Aurora had been there already that day, because she knew exactly where the latch was and opened it for Mother.

She remembered to shut it again after them too, and while she was doing it she heard that other person who was walking along the road.

'Come on, Aurora,' said Mother.

They hurried up the little path through the yard to the house, and knocked on the grey door.

'Come in,' said a voice.

Mother and Aurora opened the door and peeped cautiously in. Four children who had already settled down for the night in the big bed, sat up startled, and stared at the door.

'Why, bless me, it's you, Aurora!' said their mother. 'Come in! I wondered who could be knocking so late.'

'Do forgive us for intruding,' said Mother, 'but we were out for a walk, and the lights in the window looked so inviting.'

'And it was so dark outside,' said Aurora, 'and we could hear someone coming after us.'

'You must sit down,' said the farmer's wife. Aurora sat on the big bed where all the children were. If Socrates had slept in that bed, he wouldn't have cried and come downstairs and interrupted Daddy's dinner. Suddenly Aurora looked at Mother. They heard footsteps outside, and Aurora was so frightened that she hid her head in Mother's lap, and Mother said, 'There's nothing to be afraid of now we're here, Aurora.'

The door opened. Aurora looked up and saw a large pair of rubber boots.

'Is that you?' said the farmer's wife. 'Your meal's ready.'

'Thanks,' said the man. 'Strangers,' he said, and nodded to Mother and Aurora.

'Yes,' said Mother and returned his nod. 'Aurora came here earlier today with her father.'

'Mummy hadn't been here before,' said Aurora, 'but she's here now.'

'Oh ay,' said the man. He took his boots off, went over to the sink and washed his hands, and then sat down at the end of the table. His wife brought him a plate of steaming hot soup. The man took a spoon and began to eat. He ate very slowly, staring in front of him, and taking a piece of bread between each mouthful. Nobody spoke. The children sat up in bed and watched him as closely as Aurora.

When he had finished his soup, he nodded and pushed his plate away.

'I suppose you'll be from Oslo?' he said.

'Yes,' said Mother. 'Perhaps we ought to go now, we don't want to disturb you while you're having your dinner.'

'You're not doing that,' said his wife. 'Just sit down. You shall have some coffee when it's ready.'

Aurora was very glad to hear it, for she liked being here, and it was quite true that they weren't disturbing the man, because he didn't let himself be disturbed. He took his time over the meal, thinking about his own affairs meanwhile. Now and again he asked them a question and then went on eating. His wife stood ready the whole time, in case he should want any more.

'Where's our Peter?' asked the man.

'He's at school at his evening class again. He's got some lessons to do,' said his wife.

When he had pushed the other plate away from him, she cleared the meal away and put cups on the table.

Aurora went over to the children. For a minute or two they just looked at each other, and then they got friendly again.

'Let's pretend you're my children,' she said. 'Lie down now, and I'll tell you a story.'

'Not about trolls,' said Benedict, 'or Baby will be frightened.'

'All right, not about trolls, then,' said Aurora. 'It's rather a pity, though, because it won't be so exciting. Shall we pretend that the bed is a car instead? I'll have to get in it, then. Perhaps I'd better drive because I'm so used to it, and the road's a bit slippery.'

The children thought that was quite all right and Aurora sat by the bedpost and drove off.

Mother sat at the table and chatted and drank coffee, and when she had helped herself to cakes, the dish was brought over to the children. They were allowed to take one each.

'Aurora,' said Mother, 'we must think about going soon. Daddy must be wondering what's happened to us.'

They heard footsteps outside again, and this time it was the big boy who was called Peter. He was carrying a little torch, and Mother looked at it longingly. It certainly would have been useful to have one out of doors.

But Peter's mother looked at him and said, 'Perhaps you could go down the hill with them. It's not so easy, walking in the dark when you're strange to a place.'

Aurora could see that Mother was pleased, and she herself was even more pleased, because it would be fun now to be out in the dark. Mother talked to Peter, but Aurora said hardly anything, for she was thinking that now she would be able to get used to the dark and be friends with it.

Peter went with them as far as the entrance to the guest-house. Mother gave him a krone. He didn't want to take it, but he was pleased all the same.

'Daddy will remember about the book,' said Aurora, and that pleased Peter even more.

'Good night,' he said, and disappeared up the hill into the darkness.

When they opened the front door, all the guests were in the hall, and when they saw Mother and Aurora they clapped their hands and exclaimed, 'Here they are! They've come! Oh, what a good thing! We wondered if we ought to send someone to look for you, and the proprietress was talking of telephoning the police. We've been so anxious.'

Father was sitting on the stairs with Socrates in his arms. 'I thought you were never coming home,' he said.

'We've had such a good time,' said Mother. 'I'll tell you about it later, but you go down now, Edward, and I'll take Aurora and Socrates upstairs with me.'

The other guests kept Father company, and an hour later Mother was able to slip downstairs and sit and talk for a while too.

Next morning, Socrates woke at five o'clock again, and then it was Mother's turn to get up early. She took him off to the kitchen so as not to wake the other guests.

This happened every day of the holiday, and Mother and Father took it in turns to get up.

When they had been doing this for a week, Mother said, 'I wonder whether we can stand being away any longer. Shall we go home?'

'Oh yes,' said Father, beaming. The only one who was sorry to be leaving was Aurora. She had got very friendly with Oddmund and Arne and Benedict and Baby, and felt sad that she wouldn't be going to play with them any more. But Father said that now she had got to know them they might very likely spend another holiday here, and when Socrates was a little older he would certainly be better at staying in a guest-house.

Father went up with the book as he had promised, and then it was time to say good-bye. Aurora knew that in the kitchen they were sorry to see them go, but what was more unexpected was that the guests in the sitting-room were sorry too. The soup lady had tears in her eyes, and said, 'It has been quite an experience to have you here.'

'And we thought they weren't very nice,' said Aurora. 'Just as I felt about Nusse's mother a long time ago.'

'It's often like that before you really get to know people,' said Mother.

Socrates didn't say anything, but maybe he was sorry too. He hadn't been so restless the last night, so perhaps he was beginning to think that it wasn't too bad at 'Plum Tree House' after all.

But when he got back to Tiriltoppen and saw the high block where he lived, he smiled, and when he trotted about the flat he smiled too. But when it was time to go to bed, he looked hard at his cot, and for a moment it seemed that he might go on behaving as he had done during the holiday. However, his fingers found a little notch in the woodwork of the cot that he recognized, and all of a sudden he smiled, and grasped Lille-Rora by her nose, and lay down and murmured to himself until he fell asleep, and slept till morning.

'Do you know what?' said Father. 'Mummy's on holiday for another week. Isn't that splendid?'

It certainly was a good thing, for she and Father felt worn out after that week in the country, but when they had had a week at Tiriltoppen, they both looked well and thoroughly rested.

Aurora often thought about her holiday, and the things she remembered best were the big kitchen of the guest-house, and the dark country road, and the four children in bed at the little farm, and the father who came home to his meal.

One day when they had soup for dinner, Aurora suddenly behaved so strangely that Mother and Father stared at her. She had a faraway look in her eyes, and sat there eating slowly while she gazed thoughtfully in front of her. From time to time, she broke off a piece of bread, and took another mouthful of soup, and when she had finished she pushed the plate away.

'Well, what are you thinking about now, Aurora?' asked Father. 'Is anything the matter?'

'You mustn't say that,' said Aurora. 'You must just bring another plate and the other food, and I shan't say anything until I have eaten some more.'

'Oh, won't you?' said Father.

After a little while, Aurora said, 'Strangers, I see.'

'She's talking nonsense,' said Father. 'She isn't feverish, is she?'

'No,' said Mother, laughing. 'I think I know who she's pretending to be.'

'Who are you, then, Aurora?' asked Father.

'I guess that you're Oddmund's and Arne's and Benedict's and Baby's father,' said Mother.

'Where's our Peter?' said Aurora.